Joseph P. Bradley, Charles Bradley

**Family Notes respecting the Bradley Family of Fairfield and
our Descent therefrom**

With Notices of Collateral Ancestors on the Female Side for the Use of my

Children

Joseph P. Bradley, Charles Bradley

Family Notes respecting the Bradley Family of Fairfield and our Descent therefrom
With Notices of Collateral Ancestors on the Female Side for the Use of my Children

ISBN/EAN: 9783337306809

Printed in Europe, USA, Canada, Australia, Japan

Cover: Foto ©Raphael Reischuk / pixelio.de

More available books at **www.hansebooks.com**

FAMILY NOTES

RESPECTING THE

BRADLEY FAMILY

OF FAIRFIELD

AND OUR DESCENT THEREFROM

WITH NOTICES OF COLLATERAL ANCESTORS ON THE
FEMALE SIDE

FOR THE USE OF MY CHILDREN

WRITTEN IN AUGUST, 1883

By JOSEPH P. BRADLEY.

EDITED AND PUBLISHED BY HIS SON

CHARLES BRADLEY.

———

NEWARK, N. J.:
AMZI PIERSON & CO., PRINTERS AND BOOK-BINDERS, 30 CLINTON STREET.
1894.

I. FRANCIS BRADLEY.

Our first ancestor in this country was FRANCIS BRADLEY, who settled in Fairfield, Connecticut, in 1660, whither he removed from Brandford, near New Haven.* He, with Mr. Crane and Richard Harrison (afterwards two of the original settlers of Newark, New Jersey,) are mentioned as from Brandford in the court proceedings at New Haven, of March 25th, 1657.† Whether he was the same Francis Bradley who was alluded to in the same records, in 1650, as "Governor Eaton's man," is uncertain, though highly probable.‡ If so, he may possibly have been placed under the Governor's charge when the latter left London in 1637, with the company that settled New Haven in the following year, but could then have been but a mere boy, not more than 12 or 13 years of age. The Governor (Theophilus Eaton), was a man of great wealth and influence amongst the Puritans, having been largely engaged in the Baltic trade; and it was, no doubt, deemed a privilege for a youth to have a place in his family in order to be brought up and educated under his auspices. He maintained an immense establishment at New Haven, sometimes

---

* Savage's Geneological Dictionary of New England, Art. Bradley, Vol. I.

† New Haven Records, Vol. II, p. 208. (Vid. Appendix III.)

‡ I do not imagine that the phrase, "Gov. Eaton's man," meant Gov. Eaton's servant, as it would at the present day; but rather his protege, brought up in his family, and rather an honorable than a detractive designation. Young men intended for the mercantile profession were placed in the family of some leading merchant, perhaps articled to him, to learn the mysteries of the business, as young cadets and esquires were placed with knights to learn the soldier's art, and how to practice feats of chivalry. So that if a man could say that he was one of Gov. Eaton's men, he might take a just pride in the distinction.

as many as thirty members of his own household sitting down at his table, to whom it was his habit to administer wise and Godly discourse. An account of his life and mode of living may be found in Mather's Magnolia.* If Francis Bradley had been placed with him before he left London, he must have been born somewhere about 1625, and would have been 35 years of age when he removed to Fairfield. This would correspond with the age of his brother, John Bradley, of London, who will be mentioned hereafter. But the probability is that he came to America at a later period.

Fairfield had been settled by a few families from Windsor, Conn., in 1639, and by others who subsequently followed from Watertown, Dorchester and Concord, Mass. Francis Bradley must have been a man of respectability and some resources, when he removed thither in 1660, as he shortly after married Ruth Barlow, a daughter of John Barlow, one of the prominent settlers of Fairfield, and took his place as a freeman of the town, entitled to all the privileges of a settler, including a *pro rata* share in all dividends of the common lands. His formal admission as a freeman by the General Assembly of the Colony of Connecticut (in company with others), occurred October 13th, 1664. He had a house and home lot in the village in 1665,† and afterwards, Nov. 18th, 1672, he purchased a second home lot from one John Tomkins, with all the privileges connected with it.‡ He received from the town a homestead lot at Greenfield, in

---

* Book II. Chap. IX. Sec. 7. Vol. I., p. 152.

† *Savage's Geneological Dict. of New England.* In the Records of Fairfield is the following entry: "7 March, 1665-6, Francis Bradley purchased of William Hayden his house and home-lot of two acres and a half, bounded S. W. with the land of Daniel Finch, N. E. with land of Edward Adams, and N. W. and S. E. by highways." [Mem. of Mrs. Schenck.]

‡ "It was a law of the Colony, and of Fairfield especially, that no one should be allowed to join the settlement without a full vote of acceptance at a town-meeting. When admitted, heads of families, their wives and children, were entitled to so many acres, half acres and quarter acres, and to all dividends of lands: but each child's birth must be recorded." [Mrs. Schenck.]

‡ See Deed, John Tomkins to Francis Bradley, Town Rec. Book 2, p. 71.

exchange for his pasture lot dividend; and also one of the "Long Lotts" into which the back territory extending to the northwest bounds of the township was finally divided amongst the freeholders.* He died in October, 1689, leaving a will dated the 22d of January in that year, and a codicil without date, which are preserved in the Probate Office of Fairfield, and the will is recorded in the records of that office.† The inventory of his estate was taken the 22d of October, 1689, and his death took place probably a few days previous. He left surviving, his wife and seven children, four sons and three daughters. His sons were JOHN, FRANCIS, DANIEL and JOSEPH, and his daughters, RUTH, ABIGAIL and MARY. RUTH, JOHN and ABIGAIL were of full age, the others, minors, at the time of their father's death. I find no record of the birth or baptism of his children, except that of MARY, the youngest; but from various circumstances ascertained from the town and parish records of Fairfield I gather that the dates of their births were probably as follows: RUTH, 1662; ‡ JOHN, 1664; ABIGAIL, 1667; FRANCIS, 1670; DANIEL, 1673; JOSEPH, 1676; and MARY is registered as born December 5, 1679.

JOHN BARLOW, the father-in-law of Francis Bradley, died in

---

* The original boundaries of Fairfield extended from the east bounds of Stratford to the Saugatuck River, (?) and about 14 miles back into the country. The last purchase of the Aspetuck Indians, in 1680, was about 6 miles square, and included the old town of Norfield, the present towns of Reading, Easton and Weston. Prior to Gov. Andross' time, the freemen had divided amongst themselves a tier of home lots along the Sound, and two tiers in the rear called pasture lots. Above these a half mile of commons was laid out from the east to the west limits of the town. In the centre of this half mile of commons, one square mile was laid out to be a perpetual common forever. On this mile the Parish of Greenfield now stands. North of the half mile of commons, was partitioned to the land holders, after Andross became Governor, a series of lots stretching to the northern limits of the township, called the "Long Lots." [Mrs. Schenck.]

† Book 3, p. 267. Copy of will. The original is on file.

‡ In Francis Bradley's will he speaks of his daughter Ruth as wife of "THOMAS WILLIAMS." Query. Whether this is the same Thomas Williams of Westchester County, N. Y., who was named by Leisler as one of his Council, Dec. 11th, 1689? (See Smith's Hist. of New York; 2 Doc. Hist. of N. Y. 45.) Westchester County adjoined Fairfield County, and at that period there was an intimate relation between Connecticut and New York, and mutual assistance given in war with the Indians.

1674, and by his will, * dated 28 March, 1674, after giving to
his wife, Ann, the use of all his property during her life, he
gave the residue to his son John Barlow, and to his daughters,
Elizabeth Frost, Martha Beers, Deborah Sturgis, Isabella
Clapham and Ruth Bradley, equally to be divided between
them. There being some dispute about the division of the
property, a compromise was effected between John Barlow, Jr.,
and his brother-in-law, Francis Bradley, and others, by his
agreeing to pay them each £36.

Francis Bradley, by deed, dated August 18th, 1687, set off
to his eldest son, John, his portion of his own estate, described
as follows : " One parcel of land with all the housings, barn
and fences there on said land is, and that Francis Bradley had
of the town of Fairfield, lying in the Mile Common so called
(*i. e.* Greenfield) ye which he hath given to his son John as a
home forever : said Francis had said land of the town in exchange for his pasture lot ; said land is bounded on all sides
with the Common ; said John is to enter possession immediately after his father's decease ; also said Francis by said
deed hath granted to his son John one fourth part of his perpetual commons in said Fairfield, to possess it immediately
after said Francis his decease : further in said deed is declared
ye said John may possess one-half of ye above mentioned
premises when he shall marry." (This record was entered 18
Sept., 1689. Record Book A, p. 357.) By a deed dated
Aug. 19th, 1687, John Bradley accepted the above gift as his
share of his father's estate. (Book A, 236.)

This transaction shows that Francis Bradley must then have
become advanced in years. Men do not usually set off their
children's shares until they have become so old as to feel the
burden of taking care of their property, and to desire to see
their children established. It also raises the probability, that
as soon as John Bradley did marry, he made his home on the

* John Barlow's will, Prob. Records. Book 2, p. 77. Admitted to probate Nov. 3,
1674. Inventory, Jan. 9, 1674-5, £101.

homestead thus given to him by his father, in Greenfield, where his descendants were afterwards found.

By a deed dated 21 January, 4th year of his Majesty's reign, *Anno Domini*, 1688 (1688-9), Francis Bradley gave to his three sons, Francis, Daniel and Joseph, all his lands viz.: to Francis, "the one half of the home lott, which I bought of John Tomkins, bounded N. E. with ye common highway, S. E. with the highways, on the S. W. with Samuel Adams his land, on ye N. W. with the said lot. Also I give him one third part of all my lands I have in Fairfield except only my home lott and one half the lot I bot of Tomkins, and one acre of meadow at the beach, and one third part of all the privileges and appurtenances. To Daniel, the other half of the Tomkins lott, and one third of the residue, etc.

To Joseph Bradley, my home lott with all the housing that is thereupon, he paying unto his sister, Mary Bradley, ye sume of 25 pounds, and one third of all lands in Fairfield." [See Town Records, Book A, p. 628.]

This deed, it will be observed, is dated the day previous to the date of the will, and was perhaps made to obviate all objections as to the transmission of the title; though, the will may have been an after-thought.

It will be seen from the above conveyances that Francis Bradley provided for each of his sons a homestead. To John he gave the homestead lot at Greenfield, which, if the same that John lived on at the time of his death, contained 18 acres of land. To Francis and Daniel he gave the homestead he purchased of John Tomkins, and divided it equally between them. To Joseph he gave his own homestead in Fairfield, charged with a legacy of £25 to Mary. This shows providence as well as ability to carry out his views.

The following is a copy of Francis Bradley's Will:

" In the name of God, Amen. I, Francis Bradley, Sen'. of Fairfield, in the County of Fairfield, in New England, being weekly in body, and not knowing the day of my death and disolution, yet of sound and perfect memory and understanding, doe make and ordaine this as my last will and testament, abbergating and making of none effect all other and former wills whatsoever made by me :

Imprimis : I give and bequeath my soule unto the hands of my mercyfull Creator and redemer, hoping by the alone merits of Jesus Christ my Savore to have the pardon and remission of all my sins : and my body to be comly Intered a cording to the decresion of my Executors hereafter mentioned, hoping for a joyful reserrection at the greate day : and for that temporal estate that it hath pleased God in his grace to bestow upon me, I Disspose of as followet after just Debts and funeral Charges are first Disscharged : I give unto my Loveing wife Ruth Bradley, the sum of ten pounds, to be paid her out of my moveable estate, besides the use of one third part of my Lands during her widowhood, as I have appointed my sons to alow her, also I give her the use of one third part of all my moveable Estate dureing her widowhood.

Item : I give and bequeath unto my loveing son John Bradley six pence, I having formerly given him his portion.

Item : I give and bequeath unto my Loveing sonns, viz. Francis, Daniell and Joseph Bradley all my remaining Estate, to each an equal proportion ; and my will is that my two sons Francis and Dan¹¹ shall pay unto their Sisters, Ruth the wife of Thomas Williams, and Abigall Bradley, the sum of forty pounds to each one of them, an eaqual proportion, to be payed them within five years after my sonns shal attaine their respective age of twenty one years : my will is that my sonns shal receive their portions when they attaine their respective age of twenty one years: and I doe desire and apoint my wel beloved sonn John Bradley and Eliphalet Hill to be Executors of this my Last will and testament ; and that this is my Last will and testiment I have hereunto set to my hand and seale this 22 day of Jeneuary, in the fourth year of his majesties reigene, Annoque Domini, 1688 * (the words) my sonns), and (seal) was interlined before signed.

FRANCIS BRADLEY.

{ WAX }
{ SEAL }

Signed, Sealed in presence of us as witnesses,

> Joseph Frost,
> Eliphalet Hill.

* [1688-9] is meant.

[Endorsed on the will is the following Codicil—not signed and not recorded] :

" I, Francis Bradley, being yet of sound memory and understanding doe make this alteration or adition to my above will, which is, that my sonn Joseph Bradley shall pay to my Daughter Mary Bradley the sume of twenty five pounds within five years after he shall possess his portion, and my will is that my two sonns Francis and Dan^u Bradley shall pay to their two sisters as is above said, in this, five years after they shall possess their respective portions. In witness whereof I have hereunto set my hand and seal this—"

The following is a decree of probate :

" The will and Inventory of Francis Bradley of Fairfield Deceased was this 5th of November, 1689, exhibited to this court; and the court aproveth of them and so order them to be recorded : ye aprobation is with this Caution, that ye widow, the relict of s^d Francis shall have ye use, according to law, of one third part of ye houseing and Lands during her naterall Life : and provided also that Mary Bradley, daughter to s^d Francis Bradley, be payed twenty five pounds by Joseph Bradley her brother, mentioned in Deed of gift to him from his father s^d Francis : s^d deed is recorded."

The decree, as will be seen, does not admit to probate the unsigned Codicil, but gives it effect by reference to the deed of gift executed the day before the execution of the will. It also gives the widow her legal dower instead of the estate *durante viduitate* limited by the will.

The Inventory of the estate amounted in all to £648, a large sum for that day. It was entitled and contained as follows :

" Inventory of Francis Bradley's estate, taken ye 22^d day of October, 1689."

It.	Wearing apparel,	£3.13.0
It.	Arms and ammunition, &c., &c.	5. 7.0
It.	31 pounds puter and 3 puter pots,	3.19.0
It.	Housing and land,	361. 0.0
It.	4 oxen, 7 cows, &c.,	51. 0.0
It.	Horse flesh,	15. 0.0
It.	27 Swine,	17. 0.0
It.	Wheat in the barn,	22.10.0
It.	Oats, barley, flax, Indian corn,	18.12.0
It.	An old negro woman,	11. 0.0
It.	33 sheep, &c., &c., &c.	13. 4.0

[Recorded after will, Book 3, p. 267.]

Some years after the decease of Francis Bradley, a letter came addressed to him from his brother John Bradley, of London, who had not heard of his death. As this letter is important as showing that Francis Bradley had no other near relations, it will be inserted here in full. It is a singular fact that it stands recorded in the town records of Fairfield—the only instance of the kind. Probably the family had it recorded for the purpose of preserving evidence of their relationship to John Bradley, and their title to any estate he may have left behind him. The record is, in several places, nearly obliterated ; but by a very careful examination I was able to make out nearly all of it, and reproduce it here, placing in brackets those portions that are doubtful or entirely effaced. The superscription was as follows :

" These for his very loving Brother *Francis* Bradley of Fairfield in New England."

Here the name " Francis " is almost obliterated, but was clearly deciphered after a very careful scrutiny. The contents of the letter are as follows, line by line :

" Dear Brother :

" [It is] now near 10 years ago since I received A l[etter from you]
" tho I have [seen]* several seamen since, but noe [one y' co'¹ tell me]
" whether you are in y' Land of the Living, as I am wh[ich]
" blessed be y' Almighty, tho in y' 7[4] † year of my age, a[nd]
" I begin to think I can by no means live long wch puts me in
" minde of setleing y' small estate I have, and I have no Children
" of my owne, nether any relation [nighe] ‡ so near and dear to me
" as yourself and your children, therefore, dear brother,
" I do hartily wish and desire y' you wear here yourselfe, if it
" were posable, y' I might have y' happynes to se you before
" I die, wth would be y' Greatest satisfaction to me in y'

* Perhaps " sawe."

† The figure which I have written " 4 " is so obliterated as to be nearly undeciphera-ble. I make it " 4 " however.

‡ The word rendered by me " nighe " is so nearly effaced that it is difficult to make any thing of it : but I thought I could discern the letters *ghe.* It may be " right," but I think it was " nighe."

"world: but if that cannot be, then I should be glad if you
"have any one of your sons that is a spritely boy and about y*
", age of 16 or 17 years, that hath been pretty well bred, to bind
"him over to me, and I will take care of him. If this come to y*
"hand, be sure to let me here from you. I send it on [per] adventure
"according to your last directions, to Mr. Willson of New York.*
"You may direct to me at my house in Red Lyon street near
"y* Cross keys in Holburn : this is all at present, but to let
"you know y* I am, Dear ser, your most affectionate brother.

"JOHN BRADLEY."†

"London, Jan'y 24, 1695." [1695–6.]

* ["Mr. Willson of New York."] This was undoubtedly Ebenezer Willson, a New
York merchant of eminence. He was one of 36 merchants and principal inhabitants who
sent an address to King W. and Queen M. in 1690 (N. Y. Col. Doc. III. 749) ; to William
in 1700 : (IV. 624) ; and to Ann in 1705 (IV. 1135). He was disliked by the Leisler
party, and seems to have been Sheriff in 1697, and was displaced by Gov. Lord Bellomont,
who complained much of him for smuggling East India goods, and getting valuable con-
tracts for the excises, &c. (N. Y. Col. Doc. IV. 377; 379; 418.) Bellomont says he had
joined with the Jacobites (IV. 380). He was a vestryman of the English Church (IV. 528);
Mayor of the City 1710 (V. 168) and a member of Assembly 1722 (V. 683). Brooks, at
one time Collector, boarded with him, and was very intimate with him 1695-6, &c. In
Bellomont's letter of Sept. 21, 1698, he is called "Capt. Willson."

† In the New England Geneological Register, Vol. I. p. 379 (1847), are given the
Invoices and Letter of Instructions accompanying the ship John and Sarah, Capt. Greene,
Master, which sailed from London for Boston, November, 1651, with 272 Scotch prisoners
(probably taken at the battle of Dunbar) and sent to New England for sale—consigned to
Thomas Kemble of Charlestown. Their names are given. Amongst the consignments
sent with the ship was the following :
"S. G. R. No. 1. two trusses of goods for planters (goods intended for planters are
free of duty. I. Scobell, 113.) ship't 8th November, 1651, mark't and numbered as in the
margent. [Signed] JONH BRADLEY, SR.
[With the arms of the Commonwealth.]

[Entered and recorded at the request of Thos. Kemble, 14 May, 1652, per Edw.
Rawson, Recorder.]

I formerly thought this John Bradley, Sr., may have been the father of John, who
wrote the letter in 1696, and of our Francis : but I have since obtained a copy of John
Bradley's will, dated 12 July, 1658, which only mentions his "brother Thomas Bradley of
Thoyden Boyes in Essex," and his said brother's children—but no John—some of them
under age. He makes his loving wife Johanna Bradley sole executrix. He could not have
been the father of John and Francis. He describes himself as "merchant tailor, London."

In the latter part of the 17th Century three different persons by the name of Bradley,
resided in London, of whom mention is found in the Law reports. In 1663, one Bradley
(no doubt John Bradley, Jr., the writer of the letter) had difficulty with his wife, who carried away his bonds and other writings. To get them back he procured a friend to sue

himself and his wife in an action for taking away goods by the wife, being bonds and other writings. Bradley appeared to the suit and confessed the action; but the judgment was set aside. The court, however, ordered the wife to deliver up to her husband the bonds and papers she had carried away; but refused to bind him to the peace, because as husband he had a right to chastise her. The Bishop of London had certified at the last term that he beat her, but that she provoked him; and that by reason of their wilfulness, he could not end their differences. (I. Keble, 637.)

The difficulties between John Bradley and his wife probably produced an early divorce *a mensa et thoro;* which was the cause of his having no children, as stated in his letter of 1696. A case is reported in I. Lutwyche, 17, in which John Bradley, in 1686, sued one Edward Glynne in debt for £100, on an obligation dated 1674. Glynne set up in defence that Bradley was under sentence of excommunication, and therefore could not bring a suit in the courts. In support of his plea he set out a copy of the writ of *Excommunicato Capiendo,* issued against Bradley in February, 1686, in which it was recited that the judges delegates had certified that in an appeal pending before them between John Bradley, gentleman, and Cecilia his wife, it appeared that the said John was in contumacy before the judge *a quo* for not paying to the said Cecilia his wife, £5 costs and £8 additional costs and £23 for alimony (clothing excepted), and £23 more for alimony, and £15 for alimony, and £15 for alimony, and £22 remaining, of £35 for expenses of suit theretofore taxed—in all amounting to £121; and for this he was excommunicated by the delegates: therefore the Sheriff of Middlesex was commanded to arrest his body, and he not being found in that county, an *alias* and *pluries* were issued, and proclamation made against him, &c. The plea was overruled for defect of form, and because it was not accompanied by the judges' certificate, and the defendant was ordered to answer over.

This proceeding shows that John Bradley and his wife did not cohabit together, and that they had been divorced for some time; and that a state of much bitterness existed between them; which was no doubt the reason that John Bradley allowed the alimony to run in arrear. As he is called in the process John Bradley, gentleman, he was very likely an attorney or barrister. His ingenious proceeding in 1663 for getting his bonds and papers out of his wife's hands favors this supposition. None but an acute lawyer would have conceived it. The location of his house in Red Lyon Street, Holborn, not far from Lincoln's Inn, and still nearer to Gray's Inn, also looks in the same direction.

Besides John Bradley, the law reports mention a Joshua Bradley and a Thomas Bradley as living in London in the time of James 2d. Joshua Bradley in a suit against one John Gill, in 1688 (I. Lutwyche, 69), describes himself as one of the clerks of Wm. Tempest, Esq., one of the Prothonotaries of the Court of Common Please, and as such clerk sues by bill of privilege. Thomas Bradley, as appears by a suit pending between his sons Thomas and Richard in 1690 (2 Vernor, 163), died about 1688 or 1689, leaving a will dated in 1688, in which he devised to his eldest son, Richard, some copyhold estates at Mile end, charged with a legacy given to his son Thomas; and this was the subject of the litigation between them. But these persons do not seem to be any near connections of John Bradley. At least we have no evidence of it.

In James I's time (1611) one Elizabeth Bradley brought an appeal of murder against one Banks for killing her husband Francis Bradley in October, 1608. But this seems to have transpired in the County of York, as Banks had been tried in that County on an indictment for the murder, and had been convicted of manslaughter and taken the benefit of clergy. The name, Francis, is a slight circumstance indicating that he may have been the grandfather of John, of London, and Francis, of Fairfield. (Yelverton, 204.)

See Tomlin's Repertorium Juridicum, nom. "Bradley."

This letter suggests several observations with regard to Francis Bradley. And, first, the age of this brother, John, 74, would carry back the time of his birth to 1622, and makes the birth of Francis (about 1625) very probable. Secondly, it shows that Francis had no near relation but this brother, John ; and, therefore, that if he was at all related to the Bradleys of New Haven (William Bradley and his brothers) it was not a near relationship.* They may possibly have been cousins. William Bradley is called "Brother Bradley " in the early New Haven records, and took the oath of fidelity on the 5th of August, 1644, Governor Eaton and others having taken it on the 1st of July preceding. He (William) probably came to New Haven in 1644 with his step-mother and her children. They were not of the company that came with Eaton to this country in 1637, as their names are not in the list of first settlers. It is probable that they had belonged to Rev. Mr. Davenport's congregation in London. The father of John and Francis Bradley also probably belonged to the same society, and very likely he and the father of William were brothers or cousins. Eaton and Davenport were intimate friends, and the former was Davenport's strong supporter.

* William Bradley was the eldest of that (the New Haven) family and was half-brother to Daniel, Joshua, Nathan, Stephen and Ellen, some of whom were not yet born at the time of the settlement of New Haven (1638), so that their father and mother must have been in the company of Eaton and Davenport, or the family must have come over at a later date. Daniel was the eldest of the younger children, and was drowned in attempting to cross the river on horse back in Dec., 1658. He took the oath of fidelity 7 Feb., 1657, and was born probably in 1634. Joshua was born in 1636, Nathan in 1638, Stephen in 1642. William married Alice Pritchard in 1645, and died in 1691. He left a will in which all his children are mentioned, viz.: Joseph who was baptized Jan., 1646; Martha, Oct., 1648; Abraham, Oct. 24, 1650; Mary, Sept. 30, 1653; Benjamin, April, 1657; Esther, Sept. 29, 1659 ; Nathaniel, Feb. 26, 1661 ; Sarah, Jan. 21, 1665. Joseph had a son Joseph, born Feb. 15, 1678, and a son Samuel, born Jan. 3, 1681. Abraham had a son Daniel, and this Daniel had a son Moses, who was the father of Hon. Stephen R. Bradley, one of the first senators from Vermont, whose son Hon. William C. Bradley, resided in Brattleboro. Stephen, one of the original children, (b. 1642) was the ancestor of the Bradleys of Washington, D. C., through Abraham. b. 1674 ; Abraham 2d, b. 1702 ; Abraham 3d, b. 1731 ; Abraham 4th, b. 1767 ; which last was the father of Joseph H. Bradley and his brothers. [New Haven Records, and various other sources, private as well as public.]

The fact of the two Bradley families being of the same society would explain why young Francis was placed in Mr. Eaton's charge, and why William Bradley joined his colony in New England. Thirdly, the letter shows that John Bradley was a man of respectability and piety; and that he had looked with interest to the career of his brother in America. His desire to see him before he died, shows a warm fraternal affection, as likewise does his wish to make Francis, or one of his sons, the inheritor of his property. If a son is sent to him, he wants him "spritely and well bred;" that is, a bright youth and well instructed. This indicates in a manner his own condition in society, since to succeed him, he wants one who has intelligence and some degree of cultivation.

The result of it all is, that Francis Bradley came from London, either with Gov. Eaton in 1637, or when the New Haven Bradleys came from there (1644). That he was probably a cousin of theirs or other relative; but that his only near relation was a brother, John, who remained in London, residing in his own house in Holborn: that Francis was placed by his father (or mother, if his father were not living) with Mr. Theophilus Eaton, a friend of the family, to be brought up under his auspices.

We are groping very much in the dark, it is true; but these are *scintillas* of light which give some glimpse into that long past.

From what county of England the family originally came to London we have no means of ascertaining. Bradleys abounded in many counties, and the name is found, both as applied to persons, and parishes, towns and vills, as far back as Doomsday book. It was an Anglo-Saxon name indigenous to the soil—meaning Broad-Lea; *i. e.* Broad Land, Broad Country, &c., something the same as the French Long-champe.

In one of the Bradley families at Greenfield (a branch of Francis Bradley's descendants), is a coat of arms, in which the

Bradley and Wakeman escutcheons are combined. The Bradley is a chevron sable on a field argent, (*i. e.* a black chevron on a white field or ground) with the bust of a helmed knight for a crest. The field is unoccupied except as crossed by the chevron. The following is a sketch of the coat of arms here referred to :

" He beareth argent, a chevron sable, by the name of Bradley.
Second : Vert. a saltire wavy, ermine, by the name of Wakeman."

Some of the William Bradley family of New Haven (I have heard) have a shield gules, containing a chevron *arg.* between three boars' heads couped, *or*, with a boar's head couped gules, langued and dentated, *or*, for a crest. (See Note A. p. 61). But I have not much faith in these American escutcheons. They are often borrowed from books, and got up by flattering artists to gratify a little family pride.

Mrs. E. H. Schenck, of Southport, near Fairfield, who is engaged on a history of the town, has a fancy that Francis

Bradley was the son of Rev. Thomas Bradley, once Chaplain
to Charles I., and in 1665 prebendary of York Cathedral.
But I do not see how this can well have been. A Chaplain
of Charles I. would hardly have entrusted his son to the charge
of the Puritan, Theophilus Eaton. So far as age is concerned,
Francis might have been the son of Rev. Thomas Bradley;
and a son of his, by the name of Thomas, went to Virginia as
a merchant; and a daughter married Daniel Godfrey. The
suggestion has a phase of possibility; but I can hardly deem
it probable. We have no information that the Rev. Prebendary had a son *John:* and yet Francis's brother John was the
only near relation that he (Francis) had in 1696.* There is
considerable reason to believe that he belonged to the
Coventry family, whose pedigree is given in the Appendix,
No. I, p. 65.

* Mrs. Schenck's notion came from a memorandum in possession of Mr. Henry
Bradley of Greenfield (who died July 23, 1883,)—copied by him from a heraldic publication
in Astor Library, no doubt Wm. Dugdale's Visitation of Co. York, 1665-6, published by
Surtees Society as Vol. 36 of their publications, 1859. On p. 8 of that work is found as
follows :

"Osgod crosse Wapentake, Pontfract, 7 Aug. 1665. BRADLEY OF ACKWORTH.
Arms; Or, a fess azure, between 3 buckles gules.

" 1. JOHN BRADLEY, of Co. York, an ensign in K. Hen. 8's army to Bulloigne, France.

  2. HENRY BRADLEY, son of preceding, of Okingham, Berks., died 1645, m. Barbara,
  dau. of Walter Lane, of Reding, Berks.

  3. I. JOHN BRADLEY, of Miles near Okingham, m. Susan, dau. John Feilder, Co. Soutter.

  (a) HENRY BRADLEY, son of preceding.

  II. THOMAS BRADLEY, D.D., Chap. to K. Ch. I., now preband York Cathedral,
  Rector of Ackworth, Co. York, act. 67, an. 7 Aug. 1665, m. Frances, dau. of John
  Lord Savile, of Pomfret, Co. York. They had

  (a) THOMAS BRADLEY, a merchant in Virginia, act. 32, an. 7 Aug. 1665.

  (b) SAVILE BRADLEY, fellow of Magdalen Coll., Oxford.

  (c) FRANCIS BRADLEY.

  (d) BARBARA, m. Daniel Godfrey, of Nuffield, Com. Oxon. who had 1 Daniel,
  2 Charles.

II. JOHN BRADLEY.

Our line of descent from Francis Bradley comes through his eldest son *John*, who, as we have seen, was born about 1664, and to whom his father had given his portion by deed in 1687, to have it in possession, one half when he should marry, and the remainder when his father (Francis) should die. He must have married not long after his father's death, for on the 21st of September, 1701, he *renewed covenant*, (that is, he took upon himself his baptismal vows) in the church at Fairfield, and had four children baptized—John, Abigail, Elizabeth and Ruth.* The delay in having his children baptized probably arose from his not residing in the village, but on the homestead lott in Greenfield, which had been given to him by his father. The precise situation of this lot I have not yet been able to locate. He also had one fourth part of his father's interest in the perpetual commons of the town. I do not know if this would include one fourth of his father's long lot,† which, as I infer extended across the Aspetuck river and thence to the Northwest bounds of the township. His homestead, according to the inventory of his estate, consisted of house, barn and 18 acres of land, valued at £140. Being executor of his father's will, we find on record releases from his brothers for their respective portions of the estate; that of Francis being dated 17th of March,

* Fairfield Parish Records, under date 21 Sept., 1701.

† Mrs. Schenck writes me that the mile of common did not include the long lots. These lots lay on the East and West of the mile of common. And as it seems, by Francis Bradley's deed of Jan. 21, 1689, as well as by his will, that he divided his long lot amongst his 3 sons, Francis, Daniel and Joseph, it is probable that John did not participate therein by reason of his having been provided for by the gift of other property in 1687. See *Ante*, pp. 4, 6.

1692–3, and that of Daniel, 22d of March, 1693–4.* His wife's name was Hannah, but of what family, I have not ascertained.† Besides the children above named, he had *Joseph*, who was baptized June 14th, 1702, and Hannah, baptized September 19th, 1703. Joseph (who was our ancestor), was probably born in the Fall of 1701.‡ Hannah was not born until several months after her father's death. He died in April, 1703, the inventory of his estate being dated the 14th of April in that year. Leaving no will, his widow, Hannah, and his brother Francis, were appointed administrators of his estate.§ His children were still young at the time of his death. The four eldest being all baptized at one time, the precise dates of their birth have not been ascertained; but from circumstances indicated by the records, I make the probable dates as follows : ‖

Abigail Bradley, born about 1693, baptized Sept. 21, 1701.

John Bradley 2d,	-	-	1695,¶	"	"	"
Elizabeth,	-	-	1697,	"	"	"
Ruth,	-	-	1699,	"	"	"
Joseph,	-	Fall of	1701,	"	June 14, 1702.
Hannah,	-	Sept.,	1703,	"	Sept. 19, 1703.

* Town Records, A, p. 358.

† I am now (Dec. 21, 1887,) informed by W. L. Sherwood, of Newark, N. J., that John Bradley's wife, *Hannah, was the daughter of Thomas Sherwood, Jr.*, (b. 1624) and *Ann Turney, dau. of Benj. Turney*, and *that Thomas Sherwood, Sr.*, father of Thomas, Jr., emigrated in the Frances from Ipswich in 1634, with his wife Alice, and children. (See App. *post*, p.61).

‡ It may be that he was born on Sept. 17, 1701, as suggested in a note at page 26.

§ Probate Records of Fairfield, marked " 1702–1750," p. 21. The estate was valued at £327.9.6.

‖ It was the custom in Greenfield to baptize infants a few days after their birth, and if born on Sunday, they were baptized before night. Mrs. Schenck.

¶ John must have been born in 1693. His death is entered in the Greenfield Parish Records as follows: " John Bradley, Sr., died upwards of 80, Dec. 5th, 1773." It may be that he was older than Abigail, although my reason for order assumed was based on the settlement of their respective interests in the father's estate.

Hannah, the widow of John Bradley, married a second time ; her second husband being Cornelius Jones, of Stamford, probably a grandson of the first pastor of Fairfield Church, Rev. John Jones, who died in 1664, after having been the pastor for twenty years.* At the settlement of John Bradley's estate, April 4th, 1707 (amounting to £327), the record states† that all the children being in their non-age for choice of guardians ‡ except the eldest daughter, the court appointed their father-in-law, Cornelius Jones, to be guardian for John Bradley, Elizabeth, Ruth and Joseph Bradley; and that Abigail made choice of her mother, Hannah Jones, to be her guardian. The youngest being still in her mother's care for nurture, no guardian seems to have been then appointed for her. The mother, Hannah, was allowed £25 for bringing up the children.

In the Spring of 1717, Cornelius Jones procured and recorded receipts and acquittances from the different heirs, and obtained his decree of discharge. Abigail and Elizabeth

* "*Cornelius Jones.*" In the "*History of Stamford,* by Rev. E. B. Huntington," (1868) p. 54, Cornelius Jones is said to have been at Stamford as early as 1657. By a first wife he had several children (see p. 162) born respectively, one Aug. 20, 1646; one in Feb., 1648; one (*Cornelius*) *Nov., 1649 ;* one May, 1652; and one Jan., 1654 ; their names, except that of Cornelius, being lost from the record by mutilation. In 1657, Cornelius *the elder* married Elizabeth Hyat, widow of Thomas Hyat (or Hait), and he died 1690. His will, recorded in New Haven, dated June 2, 1690, mentions son Joseph, grandchild Ruth Hyat, and daughter Mary Hyat. Joseph died before 1690, leaving five children, aged, Mary 13, Hannah 11, Joseph 9, Samuel 6, Cornelius 3 (in 1690 as per inventory). The estates of Cornelius and his son Joseph settled 1704, and portions set off to Joseph, Jr., Samuel, Cornelius, Jr., Cornelius Seely, husband of Mary, David Miller, husband of Hannah (children of Joseph). In town Register, their births are written thus : Mary, Jan. 4, 1677 ; Hannah, Mar. 16, 1680 ; Joseph, Dec. 20, '82 ; Samuel, March 1, '85 ; Cornelius, March 1, '88. From this it would seem that the Cornelius who married widow Hannah Bradley prior to 1707 must have been *Cornelius 2d*, born 1649. He took receipts 1717 when he was 68 years old. In an allotment of lands Dec. 26, 1699, "*Cornelius Jones*" is named one of the allotters. (Hist. Stamf., p. 174) no other Jones. In a list of estates Jan., 1701, Cornelius is not named ; only "Jones, Orp. (orphan) 4£os.1d." In 1709 Cornelius Jones sells to John Reed, Jr., land on Five Mile river. (do. p. 191.)

† Prob. Records, "1702-1750," p. 116.

‡ A child could choose his own guardian at 14.

signed for themselves; John signed for himself and for his brother Joseph and sister Hannah, being appointed in the place of Jones as their guardian; and Samuel Bradley signed on behalf of Abigail and Ruth.* These receipts are dated March 7th, 1716–7, except the personal receipt of Abigail, which is dated April 24, 1717. The children probably resided with their mother and step-father, at Stamford, until they came of age, unless, possibly, the boys were put out under the tuition of their uncles or friends of the family. What was done in the meantime with the homestead at Greenfield does not appear.

These are unimportant particulars, except as they tend to show the condition and surrounding in which our ancestor, *Joseph*, was brought up and launched in the world.

COLLATERAL BRANCHES.

Before proceeding to note what is known of the said Joseph, I will state what the records, so far as examined, show with regard to his uncles, Francis, Daniel and Joseph, the younger sons of Francis Bradley I. I have already stated the manner in which their father divided his property amongst them by deed of gift, as well as by will. They all appear to have died prior to the year 1719. From the date of the respective inventories of their estates, Joseph died about

---

* This Samuel Bradley did not belong to the family of Francis Bradley, but probably came to Fairfield from New Haven a few years before this time (1717). Joseph Bradley, the eldest son of William (of New Haven), had a son by name of Samuel, born Jan. 3d, 1681. Francis Bradley 2d (of Fairfield) had a son Samuel; but he was not born until 1701. The Samuel Bradley, appointed guardian of Abigail and Ruth, daughters of John Bradley, together with his wife Phebe, were baptized in Fairfield Church, May 25, 1712, and two of their children, Deborah and Anna, were baptized at the same time. They subsequently had the following children baptized : Samuel, Nov. 15, 1713; Benjamin, March 11, 1716; Phebe, March 16, 1718. The receipt given by Samuel for Abigail and Ruth was as follows : "Know all whom it may concern that I, Samuel Bradley, of Fairfield, have received of Cornelius Jones of Stamford, the portion in full that doth belong to Abigail Bradley and Ruth Bradley, daughters of John Bradley deceased, and do promiss to free said Jones from any furder demand by ye said Abigall and Ruth Bradley, as witness my hand and seal in Stamford this seventh day of March, 1716–7."

Test: Samuel Blatchley, Jonathan Bates."

19

October, 1714, and Francis in November, 1716. The date of Daniel's inventory I have not examined.*

Francis was married about 1698. His wife's name was Sarah, but of what family I cannot report. Mr. Sherwood says she was a Jackson, probably a sister of Daniel's wife. They had seven children, as follows:

Francis 3d, baptized Dec. 3, 1699, born May 29, 1699;

Samuel, baptized Oct. 26, 1701, born Sept. 29, 1701; †

Ephraim, baptized Sept. 19, 1703;

John, baptized Dec. 30, 1705;

Eleanor, baptized Feb. 22, 1708; married Benj. Sherwood, Feb. 9, 1724,

Peter, baptized Dec. 17, 1710;

Gershom, baptized Dec. 7, 1712.‡

Francis Bradley died intestate. The inventory, which was taken Dec. 4, 1716, amounted to £881.§ His widow, Sarah, survived him.

* On April 12, 1721, the court made the following order: "Whereas it being certified that part of the Long Lott that was laid out to Francis Bradley, Sen'r, late of Fairfield, dec'd, yᵗ has not been as yet divided to the heirs of sᵈ dec'd viz.: Francis, Daniel and Joseph Bradley, who are also dec'd, the Court appoints Peter Burr and Sergt. Gideon Allen to assist the guardians of the Orphans of said Francis, Daniell and Joseph Bradley, to divide said lott (viz.) to the children of each of the above an equal share. Also to make distribution of the estate of Francis, Jr., amongst his children, &c. [Prob. Rec. 1716-35, fol. 4.]

Sept. 1, 1721. The Commissioners reported—dividing as follows: to the heirs of Francis yᵉ son, one third part on yᵉ east, next to John Tomkins: to the heirs of Dan'll one third part next to the former: to the heirs or assigns of Joseph Bradley yᵉ remaining third part—each part to be ⅓ of the width and going back the whole length.

The Commissioners also sub-divided Francis's share, and divided all his estate amongst his 6 sons and 1 daughter: Francis, Samuel, Peter, Gershom, John, Ephraim and Hellena. [Prob. Records, "1724-49," fol. 59.]

† Samuel's marriage record gives the date of his birth as September 29th, 1702, but this is evidently an error, since the record of his baptism is dated Oct. 26, 1701.

‡ Parish Record of Fairfield.

§ Prob. Records, "1716-1735," p. 4.—[In the record of deeds is the following: "16 March, 1693. Francis Bradley purchased of John Burret of Stratford and James Omstead of Norwalk, one parcel of land in Fairfield, being the long lot of Thomas Barlow's heirs, Phebe and Deborah Barlow, being 15 rods, or less, bounded N. E. with the land of John Buckley, and S. W. with the Commons." [Mrs. Schenck.]

20

Daniel Bradley, third son of Francis I., married Abigail Jackson, daughter of Joseph Jackson, and they had the following children :

Daniel, baptized Jan. 15, 1699 ; } Both seem to have died
Mary, baptized March 9, 1701 ; }   young.
Martha, baptized October 4, 1702 ;
Daniel, baptized June 11, 1704 ; married Esther Burr, sister of Rev. Aaron Burr (Greenfield Records).
Abigail, baptized May 19, 1706 ;
Eunice, baptized May 30, 1708 ;
Mary, baptized May 17, 1710 ;
James, baptized May 11, 1712.*

Daniel Bradley's estate was distributed amongst his children, March 26th, 1724; the real estate as follows : †

1. To Daniel, the eldest son, "more in the Long lott over the brook, one third part of the North end (£15), more in Sherwoods lot running ye whole length.

2. To James, "in the long lott, beginning at the brook so running upward and to be two thirds of the s^d lott.

3. To Martha, eldest daughter, a part of the long lott that was Sherwood's, adjoining to Thomas Hanford's land.

4. To Abigail, do. do. adjoining Martha's.

5. To Eunice, the fourth part of Long Lott over Sasco river and part of long lott that was Sherwood's.

6. To Mary, a fourth part of long lott over Sasco river, and part of long lott that was Sherwood's.

* Parish Records of Fairfield.

† Probate Records, "1724-1749," p. 83.

21

Joseph Bradley, fourth son of Francis Bradley I., married Eleanor—— family name unknown. He had the following children :

Sarah, baptized Feb. 3, 1706; } Joseph renewed covenant same
Deborah, " " " } day. Deborah died young.
Mary, baptized May 12, 1706 ;
David, baptized May 2, 1708 ;
Joseph, baptized April 8, 1711 ; ⟨
Nathan, baptized October 18, 1713.*

Joseph Bradley, son of Francis, as before stated, died in October, 1714. The inventory of his estate was taken Nov. 1, 1714,† £283.9. House and barn and 8 acres of land £110. 6 acres land £36. 2½ a. meadow £12.10. Part of long lott over Sasco river, ⅓, £3. ⅓ part of Long lott, £7. The widow, Ellinor, was appointed administratrix. She presented her account March 28, 1716, and was allowed £30 for bringing up the two youngest children.

Order of distribution : Widow, ⅓ land for life, ⅓ moveable absolute. Eldest son a double portion, the rest equal single portions. Samuel Bradley‡ was appointed guardian of Sarah, Mary and David ; the widow, guardian of Joseph and Nathan.

Joseph Bradley's estate was divided amongst his children in 1729, by Gideon Allen and Gershom Bulkley : to David,

* Parish Records of Fairfield.

† Prob. Records, " 1702-1750," p. 292.

‡ This was the same Samuel Bradley before referred to as guardian of Abigail and Ruth Bradley, daughters of John. Before he was appointed guardian in the present case, Mrs. Schenck says that Hillenah Bradley, a son of Francis 2d, had been appointed, and had died. But I find no record of any such son of Francis 2d, nor of any such man. If there was such a man, he must, like Samuel, have been a fresh emigrant from New Haven, or some other place ; for Francis 1st had no such son ; and none of his sons had, so far as I can discover. If appointed a guardian of minors in 1714, he must have been born as early as 1690 at least.

Joseph and Nathan, for whom widow Eleanor appeared;
Sarah and Mary, appearing by Samuel Bradley.

To Joseph, *inter alia* part of a long lott over Sasco river:

To Nathan, " $\frac{1}{3}$ part of a Long Lott on y^e East side
of the Mile Common.*

The foregoing divisions of property will help to show the
location of the descendants of John Bradley, which was, generally, North and Northwest of Greenfield.

* Prob. Records, "1724-49," fol. 76.

III. JOSEPH BRADLEY, 1st.

Joseph Bradley, son of John (before referred to as our ancestor) resided on a farm situated on the Aspetuck, about three miles northwest of Greenfield, and six miles north of Saugatuck (now Westport). In 1851 I visited the spot in company with his grandson, Joseph Bradley, who was my grandfather, then 80 years of age. Although his grandfather died the year before he was born, yet he knew the place in his boyhood, and learned all about it from his own father, who was brought up there, as he himself was brought up in the immediate neighborhood. My grandfather told me that there were many of the name (Bradley) cotemporaries of his father (*i. e.* during the middle of the last century) living all around there. About two miles north of Greenfield Hill were John Bradley, Seth, Abel, Enos, Ephraim and Moses. About one mile south of Weston, on the old road to Saugatuck, were Francis, Thaddeus, Nehemiah and Gershom, sons of " old Francis,"—by whom was meant, undoubtedly, Francis 3d, grandson of the first Francis. About three quarters of a mile south of Weston Church, were Gershom and Jonathan, sons of " old Gershom," by whom I suppose was meant the youngest brother of Francis 3d ; and at Greenfield Hill, were Hadad, Medad and Eldad Bradley, these names being remembered, probably, on account of their singularity and similarity of sound.

Joseph Bradley, son of John, above referred to, who was my great-great-grandfather, was born, as before stated, probably in the Fall of 1701. He was baptized at Fairfield, June 14th, 1702. On the 20th of June, 1724, he was married to Olive Hubbell, daughter of Samuel Hubbell, Junior. This is shown

both in the town records of Fairfield, and in the parish records
of Greenfield Hill. As he resided, after becoming settled in
life, in the district afterwards called Weston, about four or
five miles northwest of Greenfield Hill (which was that much
nearer to him than Fairfield), when the Greenfield parish
(called the Northwest Parish) was organized, and a minister
was settled there, he and his wife formed a connection with
that church. The parish was organized in 1725, and Rev.
John Goodsell was settled as first minister there in 1726 ; and
in the parish records of Greenfield it stands recorded, that on
the " 18th of June, 1727, Joseph and Olive Bradley renewed
covenant." In the same book is the record of baptism of
most of their children, beginning with a statement of the baptism of the parents, thus :

" Joseph Bradley, Born—baptized Sept. 17, 1701.
" Olive, wife to Joseph Bradley, Born—baptized Feb. 15, 1707.
" The children of Joseph and Olive Bradley :
" Thaddeus Bradley—baptized June 18, 1727 ;
" Onesimus Bradley—baptized July 30, 1730 ;
" Eunice Bradley—baptized March 18, 1732-3 ;
" Ruth Bradley—baptized May 11, 1735 ;
" A daughter of Joseph Bradley, baptized June 18, 1740 ;
" *Joseph Bradley*, Born 1746—baptized Feb. 15, 1746-7 ;
" Benjamin Bradley, Born—baptized May 9, 1749."

It will be observed that Joseph and Olive Bradley renewed
covenant on the same day that their oldest child was baptized,
18th June, 1727. It will also be noticed that there seems to
be a break between the children Ruth and Joseph. There
were in fact three other children, Martha, Nathan and Isaac,
between Ruth and Joseph.* After the birth of the last child,

---

* A new church was erected near my great-great-grandfather's residence, at Weston,
on land given by him for the purpose ; and it is probable that the children, whose baptisms
are not recorded at Greenfield, were baptized in the new church. His two youngest
children, however, were baptized in Greenfield.

25

Joseph Bradley had all his family registered in the Town Records of Fairfield, probably for the purpose of preserving his legal rights as a freeholder and descendant of a settler of the Town. This record is complete, and gives the dates of birth instead of baptism, with one or two errors which are easily corrected. It stands thus: *

" Joseph Bradley and Olive Hubbell were married June 20, 1724. Children born :

" Thaddeus, May 25, 1727 ;
" Onesimus, July 17, 1730 ;
" Eunice, Jan. 2, 1732 ; [1732-3]
" Ruth, Feb. 24, 1734; [1734-5]
" Martha, Sept. 2, 1737 ;
" Nathan, July 20, 1740 ;
" Isaac, Jan. 15, 1738; [mistake for 1743-4]
" *Joseph*, October 22, 1736; [mistake for *1746*, as I know from himself.]
" Benjamin, April 1, 1749."

The eighth child, *Joseph*, was my great-grandfather, who lived to his 82d year, when I was in my 15th ; and I have often heard him speak of his mother, Olive Hubbell, and his brothers and sisters. His own family record fixed his birth as on the 19th of October, 1746, differing (except as to the year) only three days from the above record—a discrepancy which either he or his father might easily have made. The error of the record as to the year of his birth is obvious. The record was probably made from a paper memorandum handed to the Town Clerk by Joseph Bradley himself, and the Clerk in making his entry mistook the figure 4 for a 3, or simply made a slip of the pen. My great-grandfather always referred to 1746 as the year of his birth ; and that is the year stated in the Parish Records of Greenfield. It is clear, therefore, that

* Record of Births, Marriages and Deaths, p. 144.

the date in the Town Record is erroneous. The like error in the year of Isaac's birth arose probably in the same manner as in that of Joseph's. In alluding to his brothers and sisters, I never heard my great-grandfather speak of Thaddeus, the eldest, nor of Eunice or Isaac; who probably died young, as they are not mentioned in their father's will; but he often spake of his brother "Niss" (Onesimus) and of his brothers Nathan and Benjamin (the former as older, the latter younger than himself), and of his sisters Ruth and Martha, and the persons whom they married.

The memorandum in the Greenfield Record, of the date of Joseph Bradley's baptism (Sept. 17, 1701) is also incorrect. The Fairfield Parish Records show that he was baptized June 14, 1702. He probably dictated it to Mr. Goodsell from recollection merely. The date given corresponds with that of the baptism of his older brother and sisters, who were all baptized on the 21st day of September, 1701, when his father renewed covenant, and this date was probably in his mind at the time—with the slight error of 17th of September, instead of the 21st. The 17th was Wednesday, and could not have been correct; the 21st was Sunday, the day on which baptisms were always made.* The date of his wife's baptism is correctly given. The Fairfield Parish Record shows that she was baptized 15th of February, 1707-8. She could only have been in her 17th year when she was married; and her husband in his 23d year.

Mrs. Schenck thinks that the Joseph Bradley who married Olive Hubbell (and who was my great-great-grandfather), was the son of Joseph, the youngest of Francis Bradley's sons,

---

* It is probable that Sept. 17th, 1701, was the date of his birth; and that Mr. Goodsell put it down as the date of his baptism by inadvertance, or misunderstanding. His father John Bradley, renewed covenant and had his four older children baptized on the 21st of September, 1701; but it is noteworthy that his wife did not unite with him on that occasion. We may infer that she had, on the Wednesday previous, given birth to her youngest son, and that neither she nor her babe were able to be taken to the church, and so the latter was not baptized until some months later. This explanation reconciles, or accounts for, the discrepancies of dates.

and not the son of John. But in this she is clearly mistaken. Joseph had a son Joseph; but he was not baptized until April 8, 1711, and was baptized in due course after other children, and, therefore, must have been born in that year (1711). It could not have been he, therefore, who married Olive Hubbell in 1724, as he would then have been only 13 years old. The other sons of Francis Bradley, namely Francis and Daniel, had no sons by the name of Joseph—as Mrs. Schenck supposes they had. There cannot be the slightest doubt, therefore, that my ancestor Joseph, who married Olive Hubbell, was the son of John, born probably in the Fall of 1701, and baptized June 14, 1702. Every thing on the records, with only such slight slips and discrepancies as are easily accounted for, goes to prove this fact. I have been more particular in this matter, because I have long sought exact evidence as to the direct lineage of this ancestor of mine; but having no access to the records until now, have never before been able to arrive at a certain conclusion on the subject.

In the record of deeds and other instruments, in the town records of Fairfield (which formerly included Greenfield and the back country), Joseph Bradley, the son of John (whom I will designate as Joseph Bradley, 1st), had no affix to his name; whilst Joseph Bradley, the son of Joseph, was usually designated, most of his life, as Joseph Bradley, Junior, probably as well to distinguish him from his cousin (son of John) as from his own father, who died in his infancy.

The following are some of the deeds and conveyances made to these two Joseph Bradleys, as contained in the Town Records:

Mrs. Schenck refers me to the following note of a deed to Joseph Bradley in 1732 : " Joseph Bradley purchased 1 Jan., 1732, of Samuel Bradley, Jr., in the large lott belonging to the Bradley family, on the easterly side of the Mile of Common about 300 acres (?), bounded northwest and southeast by Joseph Bradley's farm land : northeast by the heirs of Daniel

28

Burr, southwest by the commons, and it is to begin about 80 rods southward from the Aspetuck river." The amount is *30 acres* in the record, instead of 300 acres. The purchaser here named was undoubtedly Joseph Bradley 1st as the location (if I understand it right) agrees with that of his farm. On the other hand, I find a deed to Joseph Bradley, Jr., from his brother David, dated 24 Dec., 1735, conveying to him by the name of Joseph Bradley, Jr., David's share "in the home-
" stead which belonged to my father, Joseph Bradley, dec'd,
" in quantity about half an acre, bounded southerly by land of
" Samuel Thorp, Jr., easterly by land belonging to David
" Williams, westerly and northerly by common land." * I find another deed from Rev. Aaron Burr,† of Newark, New Jersey, dated 3d April, 1738, to Joseph Bradley and Joseph Bradley, Jr., for " 32 acres, part of a long lott called Bulkley's
" & Burr, bounded north by John Burr, east by David
" Williams, south upon Aspetuck river, west by Joseph Bulk-
" ley ; also four acres 6 rods, bounded north by the above,
" east by David Williams, south by Danbury road, west by
" Samuel Bradley's land."‡ The Joseph Bradley here mentioned was undoubtedly Joseph 1st, the son of John, and Joseph Bradley, Junior, was the son of Joseph: and they seem to have joined in buying out Mr. Burr's land, he having then recently been settled as pastor in Newark. On the 24th of April, 1740, Joseph Bradley, Junior, conveyed his portion of the same land to Joseph Bradley.§ This tract undoubtedly adjoined the lot purchased of Samuel Bradley, and formed part of my great-great-grandfather's farm at Weston, which extended on both sides of the Aspetuck river. I find also

---

* Town Book, No. 6, p. 236.

† Aaron Burr, " son of *Daniel Burr*, of Upper Meadow," was baptized at Fairfield, March 4th, 1715-16. He was settled as minister of the church at Newark, in 1738. This piece of land evidently adjoined the 30 acres above mentioned in deed from Samuel Bradley.

‡ Town Book, No. 6, p. 237.

§ Town Book, No. 8, p. 459.

other deeds to Joseph Bradley, Junior, to wit: a deed from
John Smith Mill* to Nathan Hubbell and Joseph Bradley,
Junior, dated 10 March, 1740-41, for part of a long lott
known as Hill's lott, ten acres; † and a deed from Theophilus
Hull to Joseph Bradley, Junior, of the parish of Greenfield,
for 15 acres of land in Aspetuck neck; part of Long Lott of
Cornelius Hull, dated Feb. 3d, 1742-3.‡ This Joseph
Bradley, Junior, seems to have been a thriving and prominent
man. He resided in Greenfield, I presume in the old place
at the foot of the hill, east of the church, where his son
Joseph and family have always lived. Lloyd N. Sherwood,
who married his great-granddaughter, resides there now. In
the town records of Marriages and Births, his family is registered as follows: §

" Joseph Bradley, Junior, and Jerusha Turney, daughter of
" Robert Turney, were married Nov. 9, 1732. Children born :
" Mary, June 21, 1733; Increase, May 29, 1736 ; Jerusha,
" April 19, 1739; Elisha, May 20, 1745;
" Wife Jerusha died Jan. 16, 1746-7. Married Mary
" Squier, April 11, 1747 : Ann, born Jan. 11, 1747-8;
" Naomi, Nov. 22, 1749; Ruth, July 18, 1751 ; Mable, Mar.
" 30, 1753; Sarah, Dec. 17, 1754; Mary, Feb. 6, 1757."

[Joseph, born Jan. 7, 1759. Charity—April 14, 1765.
Greenfield Records.] ‖ All daughters except three.

The baptism of Joseph Bradley, Junior's children is registered in the Greenfield Records ; and they contain a record
of his death as follows : " Jan. 26, 1776, Deacon Joseph

---

* John Smith had the name of Mill sometimes affixed to his name, and sometimes pre-
fixed, Mill John Smith, meaning that he was a miller. There were two Joseph Bradleys,
so said Mr. Henry Bradley, one called Mill Joseph, and the other Deacon Joseph.
(Mrs. Schenck.)

† Town Records, Book 7, p. 88.

‡ Town Records, Book 7, p. 323.

§ Page 57.

‖ The two last entries are found in the Greenfield Record.

30

Bradley, Esquire, died in his 66th year," which corresponds with his birth in 1711.

I have thought it necessary to say thus much about Joseph Bradley, Junior, to prevent confusion between him, and his cousin, Joseph Bradley 1st, my own ancestor.

This ancestor I have often heard described by my great-grandmother, his daughter-in-law, who was Martha Bates, and married my great-grandfather in 1768. She said that her father-in-law was a tall, severe man, with a keen black eye, and of whom she always stood in awe; that he was a rigid Presbyterian, and did not like any thing like levity. She, herself, was brought up an Episcopalian, and was naturally full of levity and mischief; and it may be that the old gentleman did not look with a favorable eye upon the match made by his son with an idolater and papist, as some of the old Puritans regarded those of the Episcopal persuasion. When she spoke of being always afraid of him, we, of the younger generation, used to look at each other and indulge in a sly smile; for, according to our knowledge of her, she never stood in awe of any one else.

In our family traditions, Joseph Bradley was regarded as having been a large land-holder and farmer, and a man of considerable wealth for that period. But all this was undoubtedly magnified by comparison with the hard and frugal lot which our people, his descendants, experienced in a new country which was nothing but a wilderness of forest when they undertook to subdue it. He died about the 1st of March, 1770, leaving a will dated Feb. 7, 1770, and proved March 5, in the same year; * and in the inventory of his estate, I cannot count up but about 111 acres of land, valued altogether at £554.2, in addition to his movable property. Perhaps, however, this amount of land, situated as it was, within 6 miles of Saugatuck and Fairfield, and of good quality, may have been considered a considerable estate in the middle of last

* Probate Records of Fairfield, " 1767-75," p. 331.

century. Some time during his life, he gave a piece of land
on the Aspetuck river for the erection of a church, which was
standing until after the revolution, I believe; but only its site
and a few plain grave stones, scattered about, remained in
1851, when I visited the spot. It has always been my understanding that this was an Episcopal church; though, if he was
such a rigid Presbyterian as my great-grandmother supposed,
he would hardly have given the land for its erection. I am
inclined to think, however, that her ideas of his religious ex-
clusiveness were somewhat magnified by her notion of his
personal severity. The list of his lands and real estate, as set
forth in the inventory* is as follows: [After the ordinary
farming utensils, and household furniture, valued at £10.6,
old oxen £9.18, young oxen £8, &c., &c., &c., real estate as
follows :]

" Dwelling house, £15; Barn, £50, - - - - - - £ 65.00

" 11 Acres and 40 Rods of land adjoining the house, - - - 45.00

" 20 Acres and 100 Rods, below the Church, W. side of the
County Road, - - - - - - - - - 123.15

" 19½ Acres above the 3d Cross-highway, on the E. side of the
County Road, - - - - - - - - - 82.15

" 17 Acres, 55 Rods, above ye Church on the N. W. side of the
County Road, - - - - - - - - - 57.17

" 9½ Acres at the Round Hill, - - - - - - - 63.05

" 24 Acres, 2 Rods, at the Lyons Farms, S. side of the 4th Cross-
highway, in Hall's Long Lott, - - - - - - 108.00

" 8½ Acres at Lyons Farms, ye South side of the 5th Cross-
highway, - - - - - - - - - - 8.10"

[Appraisers, Nathan Thorp, Samuel Wakeman, Jr. Verified by Nathan
Bradley.]

* Probate Record of Fairfield, " 1767-74," p. 189. Taken March 12, 1770.

32

The following is an abstract of his will : *

"In the name of God, Amen : y° 7th day of February, Anno Domi., 1770.
" I, Joseph Bradley, of y° town and County of Fairfield and Colony of Conn't,
" being in a weak state of bodily health, &c., &c.

" 1. All my debts and expenses to be paid :

" Item. I give and bequeath unto my beloved wife Olive all my household
" furniture, about 10 bushels wheat now in my chamber, all the pork and beef,
" fat and tallow I have now in my house and cellar, one cow, she to have her
" choice out of all my cows, and all y° woollen yarn in my house, to be her
" own for ever, to use and dispose of y° same as she shall think proper : also
" the use and improvement of one third part of my real estate during her
" natural life, and after her decease to go to my four sons, Onesimus, Nathan,
" Joseph and Benjamin, in the same manner and proportion as I have here-
" after in this will given them my real estate.

" Item. I give, devise and bequeath to dutiful daughter Ruth, five pounds
" lawful money, and to my daughter Martha, fifteen pounds lawful money out
" of my estate.

" Item. I give, devise and bequeath to my four sons, viz. Onesimus,
" Nathan, Joseph, and Benjamin, all the remainder of my estate, both real and
" personal, to be divided among them in such proportion as that my son
" Onesimus shall have one half so much of my real estate as each of my
" other sons, viz. Nathan, Joseph and Benjamin ; and that my said three
" sons, Nathan, Joseph and Benjamin, shall each of them have twice as much
" of my real estate as my s¹ son Onesimus ; and my moveable estate to be
" equally divided to and among my said four sons, viz. Onesimus, Nathan,
" Joseph and Benjamin."

He appoints as Executors his wife Olive, and his two sons, Nathan and
Joseph.

Witnesses, Obadiah Platt, Elnathan Williams, Jabez Hull.

Before proceeding to speak of our next lineal ancestor,
Joseph Bradley 2d, I will mention what I have heard respecting his brothers and sisters.

As before stated, it is probable that Thaddeus, Eunice and
Isaac died young, as they are not mentioned in their father's
will, and I do not remember to have heard my great-grandfather speak of them.

* Recorded in Book " 1767-75," p. 331.

33

Onesimus is registered in the Fairfield Record of Marriages and Births, as follows : "Onesimus Bradley (son of Joseph "Bradley), and Emitt Cable were married August 1, 1754. "Children born—Asa, June 26, 1756." I learned from my grandfather, or great-grandfather, that Onesimus had two sons, Asa and Thaddeus ; and that he emigrated with his family, soon after the Revolutionary War, to Delaware County, New York, and, afterwards, to a more Western part of that State. I have never heard more of the family.

Ruth married Thomas Treadwell, and was long respected in Weston as a most estimable and excellent woman, notwithstanding an indiscretion in early life. At Westport in 1851, I heard her spoken of in the highest terms by an old gentleman called Squire Nichols, who had known her well when he was a young man. Perhaps the one weakness of her life, had a redeeming effect on her character. She lived to extreme old age.

Martha married Nehemiah Cable—"Miah Cable"—the hero of many a story told on Winter evenings by my great-grandfather of his early days.

Nathan settled at Saugatuck (Westport) and had three sons, Nathan, Stephen and Abel, the eldest of whom died without issue, and the others resided at Saugatuck for many years. Whether their descendants are there still, I do not know. I get these facts principally from the relation of my grandfather in 1851, on the occasion of our visit to Weston mentioned below ; though they were often alluded to in family conversations during all my boyhood.

Benjamin, the youngest, joined the British side in the Revolutionary War, entered into their service, and lost his life in some engagement. He had one son, Gould, or Gold, Bradley, who after the war became a man of wealth and prominence in or near Weston. I always heard that he had a son Burr, who became in after years, owner of his great-grandfather's old place.

IV. JOSEPH BRADLEY, 2d.

My great-grandfather, *Joseph Bradley 2d*, lived until my time. I spent a considerable portion of my boyhood with him and his wife at Berne, in the County of Albany, New York. They had given up their farm to their son, my grandfather; but continued to live in their own house, having reserved a support for the remainder of their lives. Being alone, it was their great delight to have a child with them, who could make it cheerful by his prattle, and sometimes do errands and light chores. I being their oldest great-grandchild, they claimed the right to have me domesticated with them ; and though my mother often demurred, they generally succeeded in their wishes until I got to be old enough to be of service to my father; and, even then, I often spent my winters with them, going to school during the day. Those were, indeed, happy times. My great-grandmother always had some delicacy in her pantry, which exactly suited my taste ; and, then, those delicious hours which were spent in hearing them tell stories of the olden time—when they were young! Stories of the old French and Indian war, of the exploits of Gen. Putnam—"Old Put"—as my great-grandfather often called him : Stories of the Revolutionary war, and of domestic life; the wonderful feats of strength, or agility, of " Miah Cable," and "Siah Cable," and "Elnathan Williams," and many others whose names I have forgotten. One incident related by my great-grandmother was this : In 1777, when the English burnt Reading and Danbury, upon their landing at Campo, the alarm was carried through the country by men on horseback, and my great-grandmother

living on the road by which the "Regulars" would be likely
to come, started across the fields with her little family, then
consisting of four children, in order to be out of their way.
She had not proceeded far, before she found herself enveloped
in the very ranks of the "red-coats." The officers, however, made a way for her to pass on, and she escaped with
nothing more than a little fright. Her husband was out with
the gatherings of militia which were being collected for the
purpose of annoying the British expedition.

Joseph Bradley 2d, as we have seen, was the eighth child,
and fifth son of Joseph Bradley 1st, and was born October
19th, 1746, and baptized the following February, at Greenfield
Church. His wife, Martha Bates, daughter of Elias Bates,
was born July 19th, 1749. Her father's family is registered
in the Book of Births, Marriages and Deaths, at Fairfield,
as follows : *

"Elias Bates and Sarah Platt were married January 17th,
    A.D. 1734. Children born :

"Justus, Feb. 5, 1736; (died Feb. 8, 1736.)
"Justus, July 20, 1737;
"Martha, July 20, 1739;
"Sarah, Nov. 7, 1741." †

There is some unaccountable mistake in this record.
Martha, my great-grandmother, was certainly born in 1749.
It was so recorded in the family Bible, and she always so
averred.‡ There can be no doubt of the family identity ; for

* Page 148.

† There were other children by a second wife, amongst whom I remember Elias and
Darius spoken of.

‡ There is also an error of one in the day of the month. She always supposed she was
born on the 19th of July, and it was so entered in the family record : and I remember well
that her fortune verse in the 31st chapter of Proverbs was the 19th, "She layeth her hands
to the spindle ; and her hands hold the distaff,"—which we children always regarded as
singularly appropriate; for she was wonderfully devoted to her spinning wheel, even in
quite old age.

she always said her mother's name was Sarah Platt. Her
uncle, Obadiah Platt, was her guardian; and her cousin,
Smith Platt, used to visit her at Bern within my recollection.
If she was born in 1739, she must have been seven years older
than her husband; and 97 years old when she died; for her
death did not take place till March 13th, 1836. Her mother
having died, her father married a second wife, named Tabitha;
but of what family I am ignorant.* In the Probate Records
of Fairfield † are found the receipts given by the heirs of
Elias Bates to his administrator, Gurdon Merchant, on the
settlement of his estate, dated at Reading. Tabitha, the
widow, who had been allowed £40.12s. for bringing up the
children, gave her receipt for that sum dated Dec. 10, 1762.
Isaac Read, guardian of the children of John Read, dec'd,
gave receipt for all that was due to them, dated Oct. 2, 1761.‡
Tabitha, the widow, as guardian of Walker and Elias Bates,
acknowledged as received for them £111.10s. May 6, 1762.
Obadiah Platt, as guardian of Martha and Sarah, gave a
receipt for them of £45.16s. each, dated at Reading, May 6,
1764. John Bates, guardian of Justus, gave a receipt for him
for £45.16s., dated May 6, 1764. As Martha, Sarah and
Justus acted by guardians in 1764, they could not have been
born prior to 1740.

Elias Bates was an Episcopalian, and brought up his
children as such. When my great-grandfather emigrated to

* In the Redding Church Records (as per Todd's Hist. of Redding, p. 182), the fol-
lowing particulars appear; to wit :
Elias Bates rec'd to Church membership in Redding, Jan. 10, 1745.
His wife Sarah   "   "   "   March 4, 1748. Their children
Justus, bap. July 20, 1747 ; Sarah, bap. Feb. 2, 1752.
By a second wife, Tabitha, he had, Walker, bap. Jan. 6, 1760; Elias, bap. Feb. 16,
1761, died in infancy. [See also notes of John Bates and Justus Bates and family, in Todd's
Hist., Redding, p. 182.] As no prior traces of Elias Bates are to found in the Records,
Mr. Todd thinks it probable that he had recently emigrated from England.

† "Book 1761-67," pp. 4, 5.

‡ This was probably a claim against the estate. John Read was a wealthy and influen-
tial man in Reading.

38

Albany County, and plunged into the wilderness of the Helderberg mountains, his wife carried with her, as one of her most cherished possessions, her Book of Common Prayer, which constituted the *Vade Mecum* of her long after years of privation of church services. In that old book, all thumbed and worn, I was obliged, when a boy, to commit to memory the Commandments, the Creed, and many of the prayers and psalms and offices. (She, herself, seemed to have it by heart). Irksome as the task may have been to me, I have no doubt it was good training. But the Calendar part, by which to compute days and times, attracted my particular attention. The ability to tell by those wonderful tables, the Dominical letter of any past or future year, and on what day of the week any date of birth, or marriage, or death, occurred, excited my interest in an eminent degree. In all this Church lore my grandmother, also, of whom I shall presently speak, was a great adept; and these two old ladies were my teachers in many good and noble things.

My great-grandfather left Connecticut in 1791, and settled on a quarter section of land in Van Rensselaer's Patent, in in the town of Bern and County of Albany, attracted by the advertisements put forth by Mr. Stephen Van Rensselaer after getting possession of his estate. The lands were represented as fertile and valuable, and nothing was charged for the purchase money of a hundred and sixty acre lot, which was regarded as sufficient for a farm. But, although a fee simple was given, it had the fatal condition of a perpetual annual rent—not to commence immediately—but only after the lapse of seven years after settlement. The rent, it is true, was not large, only 30 Dutch schepels, (pronounced skipples) of wheat per annum, or its value on the first of January each year.* The land was covered with heavy timber, for which there was no demand, and which had to be consumed by fire on the ground. It took years, with great labor and toil, to clear off

* A schepel contained about 3 pecks. 30 schepels, therefore, were 22½ bushels.

enough, and get it into an arable condition, to make a comfortable farm. The result, in the end, was that the rent was found to be a greater burden than the settlers could well bear; which, in long subsequent years, produced the discontents that resulted in the anti-rent war. But these troubles came after my great-grandfather's day. In his time, and when I was a lad, the farm, by much industry and economy, produced all the comforts that persons leading a plain farmer's life could desire. The family, in removing from Connecticut, took a sloop at Campo, on which they deposited all their household goods, and traversed the entire distance to Albany by water, occupying in the voyage many days. The worst part of the journey then commenced. It was the Spring of the year, and even the streets of Albany consisted of deep mud and clay which made them almost impassable, and the country roads were, if any thing, still worse ; and when they reached the borders of the Helderberg Wilderness they were indeed in sad case. But they finally reached their destination, and put up a temporary shelter, and soon a log dwelling; and commenced to clear the land. The privations to which they were subject, however, can hardly be conceived of at the present day. Sometimes meal for family use had to be brought many miles on horseback, and seed and every thing needed had to be conveyed great distances along rough and dangerous paths in the woods. It seems hardly credible, now, that such hardships were endured by the early settlers of a district so near to a city like Albany. But they had stout hearts, and they went through it all bravely, and brought out of the wilderness a smiling farm, crowned with plenty and pleasantness. As far back as I can remember, the fields were all well cultivated, and apple orchards and other fruit trees abounded. What we called the "old orchard" had sprung up from apple seeds planted by my great-grandmother herself. One of the trees, I remember, produced an early Summer sweet apple ; and the fruit of that tree the old lady always claimed the prerogative

of having at her own disposal. I need not say that, when a boy, I largely profited by this whim of hers, being always one of her most favored beneficiaries.

Of my great-grandfather, of course, I have a very vivid recollection. He was in his 67th year when I was born, and lived to his 82d year. He was a tall, strongly built man, standing six feet in his stockings. He had black eyes, and a very sweet and kindly expression; a full head of soft, silken black hair, in which were seen but a few silver threads to the day of his death. He had a small hand but strong limbs, and must, in his prime, have been a man of great physical power. In his old age, when I knew him, he made his garden his special care, and used to set me occasionally at weeding out his precious beds of vegetables. It was quite a large enclosure for a garden, and besides containing fruit trees, was surrounded by a thick hedge of current bushes. It was well stocked, I remember, with herbs of various kinds, catnip, sage, horehound, &c., bundles of which, in the proper season, were hung up in the garret to dry: and in some sunny spot, on the farm, he always raised a small crop of tobacco, to stand him in stead in the long winter season, in case his ordinary supply should happen to fail. Decoctions of herbs were the only medicines used in the family. I never knew a doctor to be called in. Though deprived of the enjoyment of church privileges in the secluded section in which he lived, except from the occasional visits of methodist and baptist traveling preachers, my great-grandfather never forgot his presbyterian training. It was his regular practice on every Sunday, to spend a considerable time in reading the Sacred Scriptures, whilst his wife devoted herself to the perusal of her old Prayer Book. An old neighbor, by the name of Harris, who lived a lonely life a mile or more away, on a neighboring farm, used to drop in on Sundays, and have a long chat with my great-grandfather on religious subjects, generally staying to dinner. I remember this old man very well, and his singular pronunciation

of Scripture Names—such as Phar-i-sees and Sadd-u-cees— and the deference he paid to my great-grandfather when the latter expounded some particular point of religious doctrine always from the stand-point of the Scriptures themselves.—If ever a human being loved another as intensely as he loved his own mother, so I loved this old great-grandfather of mine—he was so good, so kind, so tender, and so just. He died on the 24th of January, 1828, in his 82d year, of sheer old age. More than once, sometimes in the cold winter season, I have gone to his grave alone, whilst yet a mere boy, and wept bit- ter tears for his loss. His wife survived him eight years, and died the 13th of March, 1836, in her 87th year; but much of this period I was obliged to be absent, and saw her but little, being in college at the time of her death. It was always a source of great joy, however, both to her and myself, when I could make arrangements to pay her a visit, which I always did at least once a year.

Of course, these are uninteresting particulars to everybody but myself. But I treasure the recollection of them as part of my being, and cannot refrain from noting them down for the perusal of my children, that they may learn to prize "the short and simple annals of the poor," so rich in purifying and healthy moral influences. If one lesson more than another, was stamped upon my early existence, it was the sanctity of home affections, and absolute justice and charity to all. Any thing mean, deceitful or dishonest was regarded with the utmost abhorrence in our family circle, and received prompt and decided condemnation. And I trace a great deal of this moral resultant back to the pure views of life and duty which my great-grandfather and his family brought with them from the well-spring of religious life in old Fairfield.

Joseph Bradley 2d, my great-grandfather, had five children, as follows :

42

Isaac, born Sept. 10, 1769, died Sept., 1834, at Onondaga.
Joseph 3d, born April 10, 1771, died May 23d, 1854, at Bern.
Daniel, born August, 1773, died—
Thankful, born August 25, 1775, died—
Sarah, born Sept. 1, 1777, died Jan. 7, 1838, at Danbury.

Of these, Joseph 3d was my grandfather, and will be referred to presently.

Isaac married Sarah Williams, a daughter of Dr. John Williams, of Fairfield, who, when a boy, had been carried away captive by the Indians, and lived with them several years, learning many of their simple remedies for curing diseases, of which he made profitable use in his subsequent practice as a physician. Another daughter of his, a Mrs. Babcock, confided to me a specific remedy for curing cancer, the recipe for which was left to her by her father, and which has proved effectual in several cases. Isaac left Connecticut at the same time with his father, and after staying awhile at Bern, emigrated to Onondaga County, New York, where he spent the rest of his life; leaving behind him several sons, Elias, John and Orsemus; another son, Joseph, having died unmarried.

Daniel married Poll Holmes, I think of Danbury. He also emigrated to Onondaga, after residing a short period in Bern ; and left one son, Abraham, who resided, the last that I heard of him, at Syracuse. Daniel lived to be very old. I heard of him as still living when he was past 90 years of age.

Thankful married Sherwood Fanton, of Danbury, I believe, and never left Connecticut.

Sarah married Daniel Holmes, of Danbury, and died there in 1838.

V. JOSEPH BRADLEY, 3d.

My grandfather, *Joseph Bradley, 3d*, born April 10, 1771, was put out by his father with Elnathan Williams, of Weston, Fairfield County, to learn the trade of tanning, and the manufacture of leather in all its forms, shoes, harness, saddles, bridles, &c., a trade which stood him in good stead when he removed to the recesses of the Helderberg mountains. Before leaving Connecticut, in 1794, he married *Mary Wheeler*, daughter of Calvin Wheeler, of the township of Fairfield, an Episcopalian by persuasion, and of a highly respectable character. Mrs. Schenck sends me a memorandum of a marriage recorded between Calvin Wheeler and Ruhamah Bradley, July 5, 1762. She was probably daughter of Daniel Bradley 2d, and born July 31, 1745;[*] or of Peter Bradley, and born 1743. But she must have died soon after her marriage, because the wife of Calvin Wheeler, who became the mother of his children was Mary Thorp. I have a copy of their family record which is as follows :

Calvin Wheeler, born Jan. 1742; died March 17, 1831.
Mary Thorp, born Aug. 21, 1745; died April 17, 1828.

Their children were :

Calvin, born Jan. 5, 1767;
Ruhamah, born February, 1769;
Martha, born March 23, 1771; married Smith Platt.
Huldah, born March 31, 1773; married Thaddeus Gilbert.

[*] Record of Births, &c., p. 81.

44

Mary, born Aug. 25, 1775; married Joseph Bradley, 3d.
Sarah, born March 5, 1777;
Ephraim, born Jan. 21, 1779;
Mabel, born July 16, 1781;
Esther, born May, 1783;
Anna, born July, 1785.

I remember of hearing that all these children were living in 1838, and when the eldest was 71, and the youngest was 53. They were noted as a long lived family. I think it was in 1838, that Calvin, the eldest, came to Bern, from Connecticut in his sulky, to pay a visit to my grandmother, his sister. He was a man of some note in his neighborhood in Fairfield County. I have forgotten the precise location of the family. My grandmother was a woman of much sensibility and deep piety. She retained a warm attachment to the Episcopal Church to the last, though deprived of the enjoyment of church privileges all the latter portion of her life. I do not think I have ever known a more lovely example of connubial harmony and happiness than that exhibited by my grandfather and grandmother. I do not think that I ever heard the least word between them indicative of any but the kindest and most affectionate regard. It always seemed to me, that my grandfather felt that he owed his wife his entire devotion for taking her to the retired and, at first, wild hills of Bern, far away from her old home in Fairfield, where she enjoyed the affections of a large family circle, and the advantages, and even embellishments, of a quite advanced community.

My grandfather did not leave Connecticut until 1796, or 1797. He then removed to Glen's Falls, on the upper Hudson, in New York; and after spending a short period there in the pursuit of his trade, he finally settled at Bern, on a portion of his father's homestead, where he continued to reside till his death. When his father became too old to manage his portion of the farm, my grandfather took charge of the

whole, rendering the old people a comfortable support and maintenance for life; and removed to a house adjoining theirs. As before stated, much of my boyhood was spent at this old double-home. My grandfather was an industrious farmer. When he first removed to Bern, he utilized his trade so far as to erect a small tannery for the purpose of tanning leather for the use of the farm, and occasionally some for the neighbors; but never allowed it to interfere with his farming operations. He was a man of strong, hardy constitution, honest and straightforward in his principles, utterly detesting every thing mean or under-handed, and regarded religion as a thing rather to be lived than to be professed. Although he rarely missed reading his Bible for an hour or so every Sunday, I do not think I ever heard him speak a word on the subject of religion. That he kept in his own breast, and let it speak for itself in his daily life. He also, like his father, died simply of old age. One pleasant day in May, 1854, he walked four miles over the mountain roads to make a visit to my father's home. Feeling a little tired, a thing which he would never admit before, he concluded to spend the night there. The next day he returned on foot, refusing to ride; but he had to sit down and rest two or three times by the way. When he got home he lay down on his bed, and refused to be disturbed, or to take any food, and in a day or two quietly breathed his last with perfect composure, and with all his faculties about him to the last. He had never been sick but twice in his life: once, when a young man, he was inoculated for the small pox, and formed one of a party made up to retire to a vacant building until the disease had spent its force. This, however, was rather a frolic than a fit of sickness. It was in accordance with the practice of those days, before vaccination was introduced. The other occasion was that of an attack of camp fever whilst serving in a detachment of New York volunteers called out in the war of 1812 to protect the northern frontier, and which rendezvoused at

46

Sackett's Harbor. Many of the troops had been taken with the disease and nearly all had died, whether of the fever, or of blood-letting, is hard to say :—Bleeding was the universal treatment of the day. My grandfather determined that if he was attacked he would die of the fever, if he had to die, rather than of phlebotomy; and so announced in advance. He was finally taken down and became somewhat delirious, and the surgeon appeared with his lancet, and seized his arm; but my grandfather retained enough consciousness to comprehend the situation, and with a strong effort, released himself, and aimed a blow at the doctor's head, which the latter fortunately dodged; I say fortunately; for a blow from my grandfather would have been no trivial matter. The doctor left his patient in disgust, and my grandfather got well. He often told me that he was very glad he missed the doctor's head, for in his then state of nervous excitement, he really believed that he would have killed him if he had struck him. As an evidence of his great strength, I have seen him playfully seize a strong and lusty young man, and hold him out at arm's length by the shoulder with one hand, and shake him till his teeth chattered,—whilst the victim, held as in a vice, could neither release himself nor make any resistance. He was very strongly and compactly built; had a soft blue eye, and a pleasant, even gentle, expression of countenance. Unlike his father, he became gray at an early age, and in his latter years, he had but a few thin locks of hair on his head. I was always a great favorite with him, and he would frequently seduce me away from my great-grandmother, to go out with him into the fields or woods, to which I was nothing loth. He has often, when I was but a little fellow, perhaps six or seven years of age, tied me on to the back of a horse, so that I could keep him company without being overcome with fatigue; and nothing pleased me so much as when he would take me out into the "sap-bush," in maple sugar time, and keep me trudging about amongst the woods, or allow me to play about the wigwam

near the large kettles where the sap was boiling; and as I
grew larger, I could give a considerable help in my small way,
by keeping up the fires, and filling up the kettles as the sap
boiled away. But the greatest sport was to go with him on
gunning excursions. He was an expert marksman, and many
a load of game—mostly red and black squirrels—or vicious
crows or a hawk, with now and then a partridge, have we
brought home with us after a day's hard scouring of all the
surrounding woods. Netting wild pigeons was another of our
favorite pastimes. He knew by the manner of their flight
whether they could be drawn down to the snare laid for them.
I remember one morning he called me hastily to go with him,
armed with his net and stool-pigeons (of which he always kept
a stock) to a neighboring hill-side, sown I think with buck-
wheat. Arrived at the point selected by him, we soon made
our plant of net, and stool-pigeons and booth-house, and in less
than half an hour took in at one haul more than 200 birds.
They were all carried home alive, placed in an upper room
and fed with corn, until taken out by a half dozen or dozen
at a time and made into old fashioned country pot-pie. And
the neighbors did not go without their proper share of the
game.

I cannot close this rambling notice of my good grandfather
without relating an anecdote of his last years. In 1851, when
he was past 80 years of age, he and my father made me a visit
at Newark, New Jersey, where I was then practising law. It
was proposed to go to Fairfield, or rather Weston, to see the
place of his old home, which he had left nearly 60 years before.
So we went, getting out of the cars at Westport station
(near old Saugatuck.) As we approached the old place, I
said to my grandfather, "After all, it will be rather sad for you
to find none of your old acquaintances here." "I dont know
about that," said he, "I guess we shall find Elnathan Williams;
I never heard of his death." Elnathan Williams was the man
with whom he had lived when he learned his trade; and if

living still must have been well on to a hundred years old. "Well" said I, "we will see." We went straight to the old house, which was still standing, and knocked. An aged lady came to the door. We asked if Mr. Williams lived there. She said he did. "Old Mr. Elnathan Williams," we said. "Yes," she answered, "he is my father, he lives here." My grandfather looked at me with an air of triumph. "Tell him," said I, "that Joseph Bradley is here, and wishes to see him." We were shown in, the old man was lying down, and his daughter went to him and brought him into the room where we were—old—bent—heavy and feeble, and quite deaf. "Who, did you say?" said he to his daughter. "Joseph Bradley," she replied, "your old apprentice." "Oh," said he, and looking at my grandfather, and giving him his hand, "You went away to York a long time ago, I am glad to see you." Then his head drooped, as he sat in his chair ; and after sitting there for a while, he raised himself again, and said to his daughter, "Who did you say it was?" Then she repeated, and the same greeting was all gone over again. My grandfather, who in his excitement of expectation, had refused to sit down, seemed perfectly lost in amazement. He had left this man hale, hearty, stalwart, the very perfection of physical symmetry and power,—and now, here was nothing but a poor, broken, trembling wreck—with scarcely a gleam of sense or memory remaining. He turned wistfully to me, and said "Why, Josey, he has got to be an *old man*, hasn't he!" I shall never forget that picture—my grandfather forgetful that he was himself an old man, so struck with astonishment at seeing an old friend, whom he had left in his prime, bowing under the decay and weakness of age, giving hardly a suggestion of what he formerly was. And the simplicity and apparent sincerity with which he said "Why Josey, he has got to be an *old man*, hasn't he!" made a deep and thoughtful impression on my mind. We are sensible enough of the gradual failing away of others,

but how long it takes us to feel that we, ourselves, are failing as well !

My grandfather had three children :

Philo, (my father) born March 23d, 1795.
Olive, born December 30, 1797 : married John Fisher.
Elam, born January 9, 1801.

My aunt *Olive Fisher*, (who was named after her great-grandmother, Olive Hubbell) removed from Bern with her husband to Lewis County, N. Y., (the Black River Country) in 1824. They had several sons and daughters, who are mostly settled in that region.

My uncle *Elam*, remained on the farm with my grandfather until after the latter's death. He let it slip out of his hands, however, and subsequently removed to Albany, where he died several years ago. He had one son, John, and two or three daughters, of whom I have lost sight. I believe John, the son, died unmarried. Thus the old place which had been the family home for seventy years, fell into the hands of strangers, and I have had no heart to visit it since.

VI. PHILO BRADLEY.

Philo Bradley, my father, married Mercy Gardiner, my mother, when both of them were only 17 years old. I was their eldest child, and they had eleven more; in all seven sons and five daughters. The births of the several children were as follows:

1. Joseph P. Bradley, born March 14, 1813; married Mary Hornblower, dau. of Ch. Justice Hornblower, of New Jersey, and resides in Washington.
2. Emma, born May 7, 1815, married Elias Willsey; and died July 2, 1867, in Schenectady, N. Y.
3. Daniel Gardiner, born June 8, 1817; resides in Albany.
4. Mary, born July 12, 1819; married Ambrose W. Palmer; and resides in Decatur, Illinois.
5. 6. Elias Bates and Darius Bates, twins, born March 7, 1822; Elias resides at Gallupville, Schoharie County, N. Y.; Darius died when only a few days old.
7. Olive, born July 21, 1824; died Nov. 3, 1838. (Her name was in compliment to my great-grandfather—his mother's name—the centenary of her marriage.)
8. Phebe Catherine, born July 3, 1827; married John Wilshaw, and resides in Albany.
9. Elam Isaac, born April 7, 1830; resides in Albany.
10. Mercy Jane, born April 11, 1833; married Roswell O. Hutchins, and resides near Rose Hill, Mahaska Co., Iowa.
11. Theodore, born March 19, 1836; Nebraska; studied law.
12. Charles Downing, born Feb. 11, 1839; resides in Canon City, Colorado; is a lawyer.

52

My father spent the greatest part of his life at farming ; first, on a portion of his father's farm, then on an adjoining farm, in 1818, and again from 1822 to 1824 inclusive ; next on a farm on Irish Hill, about five or 6 miles from my grandfather's, in 1825 and 1826; finally on another farm on Irish Hill, about 4 miles from my grandfather's, which he purchased, and on which and a farm adjoining, he continued to reside from 1827 till his death in 1861. For about a year (1818-19), he resided at Catskill, engaged in mercantile business, which, I believe, was not a success. During several succeeding years, he taught school part of the time, and part of the time assisted my grandfather on his farm. This was from 1819 to 1821 inclusive. In 1817 he, with his father-in-law, Daniel Gardiner, took a journey, by horse and sleigh, to the ends of the earth, namely, to Ohio, in the vicinity of Columbus. My grandfather Gardiner had some lands, derived from a brother, Col. James Gardiner, a Revolutionary officer, who had received them as a portion of his bounty. They found the lands, but the surrounding wilderness looked so forbidding, they concluded to sell them. Columbus had recently been laid out as a city, but it had no houses, or very few, and the stumps of the forest trees occupied the places of the streets and lots. The adventures of this journey furnished entertainment on winter evenings for a number of years afterwards. Col. James Gardiner, and his brother Daniel, my grandfather, were sons of Job Gardiner and Hannah Howland, of Newport, Rhode Island. The father, Job Gardiner, was a commissary during the Revolutionary war; and James served in the army, having attained the rank of Colonel before the war closed ; and settled, at its close, at Wilmington, North Carolina, where he died in 1787.

Job Gardiner, my great-grandfather, emigrated to Stephentown, Rensselaer County, New York, in 1781. My grandfather, Daniel Gardiner, was born at Newport in 1767, emigrated with his father to Stephentown, and there married

53

Mercy Burtch, in 1787. A few years later he settled in Albany County, in what was then called Rensselaerville, but was afterwards set off as the town of Westerlo. There my mother was born, September 18, 1794. My grandfather, though most of his life a farmer, was a man of very quick wit, a fair mathematician and surveyor, and seemed to have a natural genius for mathematical investigations. He had a large family, and his younger boys were of my own age; and it used to be his delight to set us at all kinds of games of skill, and to give us sums to do, and problems to solve, having, himself, the most ingenious way of simplifying questions of that sort, and making them plain to our understandings. With a piece of chalk he would rapidly draw a diagram on the hearth, of a winter's evening, and explain to us the mysteries of angles and triangles, and hypothenuses, and circles, and diameters, etc., and show us their practical use. I was a particular favorite, because I had a natural aptness for such things, and he set me up as an example to excite the emulation of his own boys. One of them, Benjamin Franklin, younger than myself, became a very bright and promising young man, but died in 1838, whilst studying medicine in Albany. Another, Perry Green, who was just my age, became a skilled machinist and mechanic, and made many inventions in that department, for which he obtained scores of patents, and had amassed at one time quite a large fortune. He resided mostly in New York, but purchased a beautiful farm near the village of Schoharie, where his family usually made their home. He died several years ago. Heman, next older than Perry Green, was also an inventor and patentee, as well as a farmer. The eldest, James D. Gardiner, was six years older than my mother, being born on the 29th of February, 1788, and boasted, when 80 years of age, that he had had only twenty birthdays. In person he was tall and of fine presence. He continued a farmer in Bern through a very long life, much respected and beloved, often filling offices of

trust both public and private, in the town and in the legisla-
ture of the state. He was a religious man, a Methodist by
profession, but one of the calm and thoughtful kind, opposed
to all noisy exhibitions of emotion. He was a man of considerable reading, but of more reflection and observation, and
was one of those who exercised a very healthful influence on
my early life. Another brother of my mother's, younger than
she, was named Job, a thin, wiry, ingenious person, who was
a great thinker and reasoner on religious and metaphysical
subjects, and started inquiries in my mind which took many
years to solve, if they are all solved yet. He was a cabinet
maker by trade, but read much, and being the custodian of the
town library, he had an opportunity of indulging his taste in
that way. What delicious Saturday afternoons and Sundays
I have spent at his house arguing and talking with him, and
rummaging and poring over the literary treasures which he had
in his keeping—such, for example, as Josephus's, Rollin's,
Gibbon's and Hume's Histories! Park's and Bartram's
Travels! and a great many other books of the same sort,
together with solid books of Divinity, which formed the
country reading of those days. This was after I had got to be
a youth from fourteen to eighteen years of age. Poor uncle
Job! He died early, at the age of 37; and died as he had
lived, in the firm and calm conviction that what could not be
thought out and understood was not worth knowing or
believing!

But my mother, after all, in my own eyes, was the jewel of
that family. She was the charm of our home, gifted with
good sense, native shrewdness, sweet temper and unalloyed
goodness. I never knew her to be in a passion, rarely to
exhibit any appearance of anger. But with all her goodness,
she had a vein of keen and gentle satire which ever furnished
us with amusement, if not the immediate objects of it. And
then, her laugh, without being loud, was so contagious! And
her counsels were ever so wise, so gentle, so elevated, so full

of all charitableness! I think I have never known a more
admirable character, or one more in harmony with the principles which she professed. She was a Methodist in religion,
but, like her brother James, of the mild, and not the ardent,
type. She had the broadest charity for all, and would never
allow her children to indulge in censorious remarks about our
neighbors. She always had some excuse for their short com-
ings. I never knew her to be idle. Having a large family to
care for, she was unceasing in her efforts to make them
respectable, comfortable and happy. Her fortune-verse in the
31st chapter of Proverbs was, of course, the 18th, the day of
the month on which she was born : "She perceiveth
that her merchandize is good ; her candle goerh not out by
night." We often read it aloud to her in jest, and told her it
was exceedingly appropriate, except the " merchandize," as we
often wanted many things in the latter category which our
straightened means would not permit her to procure for us.
I have spoken of her good sense and native shrewdness. She
had the still higher intellectual gift of keen and discriminating
analysis. With no learning from books, or only such as could
be obtained in a common country school, she had a marvelous
faculty of making calculations in her head, and of unraveling
difficult questions and problems—of course, I do not refer to
questions in advanced mathematics. Many a time when I
have given up a problem in despair, and perhaps in a burst of
temper railed at the book or its author, she has quietly asked
me to read the question to her; and after a few moments'
reflection, she would so restate the case, or put such a question, or make such a suggestion, that the explanation would
occur to me at once, and I would exclaim, "Oh, pshaw ! I can
do it." And then she would add, " You must learn to be
more patient, Josey." If I have any turn for mathematics (as
some suppose, though it has never been greatly developed), I
must have inherited it from my mother. Such was the calm-
ness and clearness of her judgment, that she was always

affectionately looked up to by her younger brothers and sisters as a sort of second mother, to whom they ever resorted for advice, and for comfort when in trouble.

Such was my mother; such was my father's wife, to whom all the latter verses of the chapter of Proverbs referred to might well be applied. The fabrics that she wove on her own loom, the figured counterpanes, and table covers, and other marvelous products of the same sort—all designed and elaborated by her own ingenuity—often exciting the wonder and admiration of neighboring dames, were but the image of her daily life, into the texture of which was interwoven whatever is beautiful and symmetrical, and apposite to its purpose and surroundings.

My father, though always doomed to hard toil, was very fond of books, particularly books of history and travel. I think he must have read nearly the whole Ancient Universal History through in course, consisting of twenty thick octavo volumes. Whenever he came to a passage that pleased him, and which he thought might interest us, he would read aloud; and I remember to have attained quite a minute knowledge of the exploits of Alexander the Great and of Julius Cæsar in that way. My father's taste for reading was inherited by most of his children, and we always had books of interest at our command. We never needed outside excitements to make us happy; and, perhaps, on that account were sometimes thought a little exclusive by our neighbors. If we were poor, we were proud of our poverty, and endeavored to be content with our lot—except that, for myself, I always from my early youth, had a burning thirst for a more complete education. I shall never forget my poor father's sad and despairing look when, after a long struggle with myself, one bleak day in November, 1831, I proposed to him to let me go out into the world to see if I could not better my fortunes, and manage in some way to get a college training. He finally assented; but I saw that it was with a heavy heart; and I hope that the assistance

which I rendered him in his more advanced years, in some measure repaid him for the sorrow that I then caused. And well do I remember, also, my mother's longing look after me, as her figure stood in the door, when a year or two later I started for the distant Jerseys to enter college. I never returned to that mountain home to live; but the pilgrimages I made there once ever year as long as my father or mother lived, are bright episodes in my life. They were laid side by side in the country burying yard near by, and the following inscriptions mark the place of their rest :

PHILO BRADLEY.

Born at Weston, Conn't, March 23d, 1795 : Died Dec. 4th, 1861 :
His family out of love and respect for his memory have erected this stone over the place where his remains repose, awaiting the resurrection of the Just.

MERCY BRADLEY, WIFE OF PHILO BRADLEY.

Born at Westerlo, N. Y., Sept. 18th, 1794 : Died July 30th, 1866 :
Faithful in all the duties of life,—as daughter, sister, wife, mother,—unobtrusive, self-sacrificing, patient, truthful, pious,—she receives this last memorial of the love and reverence of her children.

In person my father was below the middle size, though compact and strong of build. His eyes were blue, his cheeks ruddy, and his hair nearly black. I have heard the old people say, that he took more after his mother's family, the Wheelers, in personal appearance, than after that of his father.

My mother was said to have been very handsome in her youth. She had a fine brown eye, perhaps it would be called chestnut colored; black hair, and much of it; and, in her mature years, a stout figure, but, when a maiden, lithe and strong. Both were gifted with strong constitutions and much power of endurance.

58

EDITOR'S NOTE.

The children of Joseph P. Bradley, to whom he addressed the foregoing pages, were the offsprings of his marriage on October 23d, 1844, with Mary Hornblower, of Newark, New Jersey, the youngest daughter of Chief Justice Hornblower of that State, who survives him.

There were seven in all, born as follows:

1. Mary Burnet, born Sept. 26, 1845; married Feb. 16, 1870, Henry V. Butler. Issue—1. Mary Hornblower; 2. Julia Colt; 3. Henry Varnum (U. S. Naval Cadet).

2. Caroline, born Nov. 2, 1847; married June 29, 1893, Jos. C. Hornblower.

3. Joseph Hornblower, born Oct. 6, 1849; died Sept. 12, 1854.

4. Harriette, born Oct. 4, 1851; died April 26, 1856.

5. William H., born Sept. 13, 1853; married Nov. 17, 1880, Eliza McCormick Cameron. Issue— 1. Joseph Gardner; 2. James Donald Cameron.

6. Charles, born Aug. 31, 1857; married April 12, 1882, Julie E. Ballantine. Issue — 1. Charles Burnet; 2. Robert Ballantine.

7. Joseph Richard, born June 28, 1862; died Feb. 7, 1864.

Four of these, viz: Mary, Caroline, William and Charles, were living when the notes were written, and one, William, has since died.

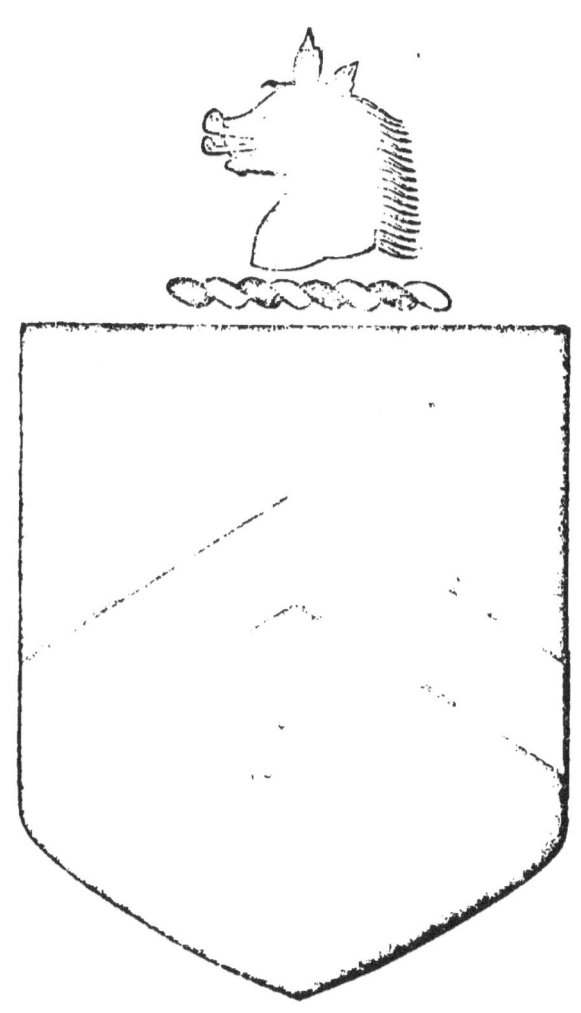

Bradley.

Motto: "Liber ac Sapiens Esto."

NOTE A.

(See ante fol. 13.)

BRADLEY ARMS.

In a letter to me from Leonard A. Bradley, Esq., of 63 Wall Street, N. Y., (July 8, 1887) he states that Hon. Wm. C. Bradley, of Westminster, Vt., many years since (1859) informed him (by letter) that when he studied law at the close of last century with Judge Lyman Strong, of Amherst, Mass., he boarded in the house of Dr. Coleman, and on the dinner table there saw a silver can or tankard, with a coat of arms engraved upon it, which was given to Dr. Coleman's first wife, Sally Beecher, daughter of Eliphalet Beecher and Sarah Bradley, youngest daughter of old Stephen Bradley, of New Haven. On this tankard was etched a coat of arms, as follows:

Shield red, with chevron white between three boars' heads couped, gilded, with a crest containing a boar's head couped, and gilded. Motto, *"Liber ac Sapiens Esto."*

Leonard A. Bradley says, that W. C. Bradley sent him an impression of a seal made from this coat of arms on sealing wax. George H. M. Bradley, of Burlington, Vt., writes me that Wm. C. Bradley sent his father (Hon. Harry Bradley) a number of impressions of this seal. George H. M. sent me one of them, from which I had a brass seal engraved. He also informs me that the *tankard* is still in existence, in possession of Mr. Philip Livingston, and he hopes to get possession of it.

This discovery seems to me to establish the connection between the Bradley family of New Haven and the Coventry family mentioned in the following Appendix, I. Of Francis Bradley's connection with the same family, I have no doubt. Nor have I any serious doubt that he was a son of Francis Bradley, of Coventry, born in 1595, as conjectured on p. 66.

APPENDIX.

I.

In The Harleian Society Publications, Vol. XII., containing William Camden's Visitation of the County of Warwick, 1619, published in 1877, and edited by John Fetherston, F.S.A., at pages 354, 355, are found the arms and pedigree of a Bradley family which has many grounds of probability of being that from which we are immediately descended. It seems to be brought down to the very fathers of William Bradley of New Haven, and of Francis Bradley of Fairfield. The next two pages contain a copy of this entry. The arms were not contained in the early editions of Burke's General Armory; but in the edition of 1878, he copies it from Camden (then lately published) and says, as follows, to wit :

" BRADLEY (confirmed by the Deputies of Camden, Clarenceux to FRANCIS BRADLEY of Coventry, grandson of WILLIAM BRADLEY, Co. York, Her. Vis.) gu. a chev. ar. between three boars' heads couped *or*."

BRADLEY.

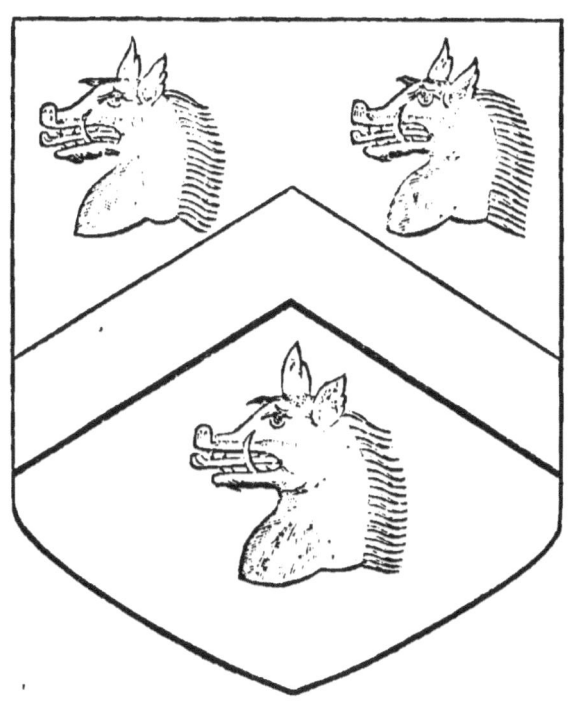

" Arms—*Gules*—a chevron *argent* between three boars' heads *or*."

65

Willm⁵ Bradley de Sheriff —
hutton in Com. Ebor.

Willm⁵ Bradley de Civitate == Agneta filia Thomæ Margates
Coventriæ in Com. War. | de Riseden in Com. Northamp.

Tho. Bradley == Maria filia Joh'is Cotes de Lakingale in Co. Suff.
2 filius. | relict Will'i Jackson, Captain of Ireland.

Francis Bradley == Francisca filia Fran. Watkins de Pont
fil. primogenitus. | Poole in Com. Monmouth in Wallia

Franciscus Bradley fil et hær. act. 24, 1619.   Anna Maria.

Willm⁵ Bradley == Johanna fil. . . . . . Waddington
3 filius. | de Com' Nott.

. . . . filius act 3   1. Anna.   3. Elizabeth.
dieru 4 Septemb.   2. Magdalena.   4. Letticia.
1619.

NOTE.

We have above—

1. William Bradley, of Sheriff-Hutton, in Co. York.
2. William Bradley, of City of Coventry, Co. Warwick,—
   Agnes Margate.
3. (1) Francis Bradley, eldest son, m. Francisca Watkins.
4. (a) FRANCIS BRADLEY, son and heir, aged 24 in 1619,
   born 1595. (b) Anna Maria.
5. (2) Thomas Bradley, 2d son, m. Maria Cotes.
6. (3) WILLIAM BRADLEY, 3d son, m. Johanna Waddington,
   and had ⸵
7. (a) Anna, (b) Magdalen, (c) Elizabeth, (d) Letticia,
   (e) infant boy born Sept. 1, 1619. Wm. must have
   married as early as 1610; born (say) 1585, ten years
   before his nephew Francis.

66

My conjecture is, that William Bradley, born in 1585, and Francis, born in 1595, uncle and nephew, were respectively the fathers of William Bradley of New Haven and Francis Bradley of Fairfield. My reasons are:

1. The family names.

2. The arms—which have been claimed by the family in this country.

3. The fact that William and Francis of Connecticut were followers and adherents of Theophilus Eaton and Rev. John Davenport. The significancy of this circumstance arises from the fact that William and Francis of Coventry and Eaton and Davenport were all originally Coventry boys almost of the same age, and no doubt brought up in the congregation of Eaton's father in Coventry. Their ages were as follows:

William Bradley, born about 1585 to 1590.
Theophilus Eaton, born 1592.
Francis Bradley, born 1595.
John Davenport, born 1597.

As Theophilus Eaton became a very wealthy merchant, and they were all Puritans, William Bradley and Francis Bradley would be very likely to place their sons with him or under his auspices in London.

William Bradley of New Haven must have been born about 1620. He may have been the very child born September 1, 1619 when the Heraldic visitors were going their rounds.

Francis Bradley of Fairfield was probably born about 1625. He may have been placed with Eaton whilst a mere boy. I suppose him and his brother John to have been the sons of Francis of 1595. Of course this is conjecture, but it has many reasons to support it.

67

II.

JOHN DAVENPORT.

(Born 1597 ; died 1670.)

In 1616, John Davenport, then 19 years of age, began to preach in London, having already preached about six months in the Chapel of Hilton Castle, near the city of Durham. In June, 1619, the vestry of St. Lawrence, Jewry, elected him Lecturer and Curate, and he labored in that church for upwards of five years. His next charge was St. Stephens, Coleman Street, to which he was elected vicar by the parishioners in October, 1624; but experienced some difficulty in obtaining his confirmation on account of his supposed leaning to Puritanical principles. Laud evidently disliked him. The communicants of his new parish amounted to 1400. In August, 1633, Laud succeeded Abbott to the Archbishopric of Canterbury; and then Davenport, having become confirmed in the principles of non-conformity, left London, and after three months concealment, retired to Holland, and a new vicar was elected by the parish of St. Stephens. For a time he preached in the English church in Amsterdam; but disagreeing with Mr. Paget, the old minister there, about administering baptism to the children of those who were not church members, he desisted after less than six months. He was particularly opposed by Stephen Goffe, a toady of Laud's, who constantly wrote to the latter about Davenport, and how he, Goffe, had succeeded in silencing him. He remained in Amsterdam, the Hague, and Rotterdam, until the end of 1636, or beginning of 1637, when he returned to England, probably as the guest of Lady Vere at Hackney, where he was reported to be by Laud's Vicar General in March, 1637.

68

In April he succeeded in getting away safely with the colony of Theophilus Eaton.

This colony arrived at Boston in two ships on the 26th of June, 1637, and remained there for nine months. They founded New Haven in April, 1638. On the 4th of June, 1639, the government was organized at a meeting of the planters, in Newman's barn, and after a sermon by Davenport, the fundamental articles proposed by him were agreed to. The place was at first called by its Indian name Quinnipiac, but after a year or two the name of New Haven was adopted. Eaton was elected the first governor, and retained that position until his death, which occurred suddenly on the 7th of January, 1658. In 1665, the colony was united to that of Connecticut under the charter obtained by Governor Winthrop in 1662 ; but against Mr. Davenport's strenuous opposition. In 1663 he published an argument against baptizing the children of those who had themselves been baptized, but who had never made a profession of their faith. In September, 1667, Davenport, then in his 71st year, was called to the First Church in Boston, and being opposed by a part of the congregation, the result was the establishment of the Old South Church. He died in Boston in March, 1670. He was a great student, and a voluminous writer; but many of his productions are still in manuscript. A very full account of his Life and Labors is given by Franklin B. Dexter, in a paper read before The New Haven Colony Historical Society, Feb. 1, 1875, and published in the second volume of its Proceedings, pp. 205—238. Mather's account is somewhat loose and rhetorical.

69

III.

COLONY OF NEW HAVEN.

PROCEEDINGS OF THE MAGISTRATE'S COURT, 25TH OF 3D MO., 1657.

(New Haven Records.—Vol. II. p. 208.)

Thomas Hopewell, an Indian at Branford, was complained of for railing and threatening words to several persons, as John Whitehead, *Francis Bradley*, Samuel Ward, Josias Ward and goodwife Williams and her son—and hath also accused to goodw. Williams, Francis Bradley for being naught with his wife, and after denyed it again, but showing no just cause for such words, he was committed. After failing again to produce any proof, only he accused the wife of Rich'd Harrison, for giving him some ill words, which he requited with worse,—at last he confessed that he had done foolishly, and said he was faulty in the particulars mentioned, and promised amendment, whereupon Mr. Crane, John Whitehead, Franc. Bradley and Richard Harrison, who were present, declared themselves satisfied so farr as to make a tryall for a time—and the court, after reprimanding him, discharged him upon his paying the fees of his imprisonment.

www.ingramcontent.com/pod-product-compliance
Lightning Source LLC
Chambersburg PA
CBHW032009010726
47493CB00007B/2333